OXFORD WORLD'S CLASSICS

THREE TALES

GUSTAVE FLAUBERT was born in 1821 in Rouen, where his father was chief surgeon at the hospital. From 1840 to 1844 he studied law in Paris, but gave up that career for writing, and set up house at Croisset in 1846 with his mother and niece. Notwithstanding his attachment to them (and to a number of other women), his art was the centre of Flaubert's existence, and he devoted his life to it. His first published novel, *Madame Bovary*, appeared in 1856 in serial form, and involved Flaubert in a trial for irreligion and immorality. On his acquittal the book enjoyed a *succès de scandale*, and its author's reputation was established.

Flaubert has been considered a realist. It is true that he took enormous trouble over the documentation of his novels—his next, *Salammbô* (1862), involved a trip to North Africa to gather local colour. But Flaubert's true obsession was with style and form, in which he continually sought perfection, recasting and reading aloud draft after draft.

While enjoying a brilliant social life as a literary celebrity, he completed a second version of *L'Éducation sentimentale* in 1869. *La Tentation de Saint Antoine* was published in 1874 and *Trois Contes* in 1877. Flaubert died in 1880, leaving his last work, *Bouvard et Pécuchet*, to be published the following year.

A. J. KRAILSHEIMER was Emeritus Student and Tutor in French at Christ Church, Oxford from 1957 until his retirement in 1988. His published work is mostly on the sixteenth and seventeenth centuries, but among his translations are Balzac's *Père Goriot* (also in Oxford World's Classics), *Salammbô*, and *Bouvard et Pécuchet*.

OXFORD WORLD'S CLASSICS

*For over 100 years Oxford World's Classics have brought
readers closer to the world's great literature. Now with over 700
titles—from the 4,000-year-old myths of Mesopotamia to the
twentieth century's greatest novels—the series makes available
lesser-known as well as celebrated writing.*

*The pocket-sized hardbacks of the early years contained
introductions by Virginia Woolf, T. S. Eliot, Graham Greene,
and other literary figures which enriched the experience of reading.
Today the series is recognized for its fine scholarship and
reliability in texts that span world literature, drama and poetry,
religion, philosophy and politics. Each edition includes perceptive
commentary and essential background information to meet the
changing needs of readers.*

OXFORD WORLD'S CLASSICS

GUSTAVE FLAUBERT

Three Tales

Translated with an Introduction and Notes by
A. J. KRAILSHEIMER

OXFORD
UNIVERSITY PRESS

OXFORD
UNIVERSITY PRESS

Great Clarendon Street, Oxford OX2 6DP

Oxford University Press is a department of the University of Oxford.
It furthers the University's objective of excellence in research, scholarship,
and education by publishing worldwide in

Oxford New York

Athens Auckland Bangkok Bogotá Buenos Aires Cape Town
Chennai Dar es Salaam Delhi Florence Hong Kong Istanbul Karachi
Kolkata Kuala Lumpur Madrid Melbourne Mexico City Mumbai Nairobi
Paris São Paulo Shanghai Singapore Taipei Tokyo Toronto Warsaw

with associated companies in Berlin Ibadan

Oxford is a registered trade mark of Oxford University Press
in the UK and in certain other countries

Published in the United States
by Oxford University Press Inc., New York

Translation, Introduction, Note on the Text, Further Reading,
Notes © A. J. Krailsheimer 1991
Chronology © Terence Cave 1981

British Library Cataloguing in Publication Data

Data available

Library of Congress Cataloging in Publication Data
Flaubert, Gustave, 1821–1880.
[Trois contes. English]
Three tales/Gustave Flaubert; translated with an introduction
and notes by A. J. Krailsheimer.
p. cm.—(Oxford world's classics)
Translation of: Trois contes.
Includes bibliographical references.
Contents: A simple heart—The legend of Saint Julian the
Hospitaller—Herodias.
1. Flaubert, Gustave, 1821–1880—Translation, English.
I. Krailsheimer, A. J. II. Title. III. Series.
PQ2246.A26 1991 843'.8—dc20 90–33068

ISBN 978–0–19–955586–4

12

Printed in Great Britain by
Clays Ltd, Elcograf S.p.A.

CONTENTS

CONTENTS

THREE TALES

INTRODUCTION

FLAUBERT's first published novel, *Madame Bovary* (1857), remains more than a century later the work for which he is most universally famous, but it was the last work published in his lifetime, these *Three Tales* (1877), which contemporary critics received with most general acclaim. Had he lived a little longer and been able to publish the much more contentious *Bouvard and Pécuchet* no such neat symmetry would have been possible. Yet it was as a distraction from what he obstinately regarded as his most important work that he broke off his labours on it to compose these tales. Moreover the most generally popular of the three, *A Simple Heart*, was written in response to a plea, or a challenge, by his close friend George Sand, who, with some justification, found the underlying tone of his novels negative and depressing. To please her, rather than from any, at least initial, conviction, Flaubert wrote the story of the humble servant Félicité as 'a work marked by compassion'. In the event such unwonted tenderness became an explicit aim of this successful work, but the powerful tensions of Flaubert's character and art were not similarly resolved in the other two tales, which thus point up in one comparatively slim volume the contrast and alternance so often noted by critics in his work as a whole.

The last decade of Flaubert's life was full of sombre events. Soon after publishing *A Sentimental Education* (1869) he found himself in a nation at war, and put on uniform as a reservist. The Prussian army occupied his home at Croisset, near Rouen, and relief at their departure was soon tempered by grief at his mother's death in 1872. The much reworked *Temptation of Saint Antony* finally appeared in 1874, but the following year Flaubert came near to financial ruin through trying in vain to save the husband of his adored niece Caroline from bankruptcy. Faced with so much grief and disappointment he found progress on *Bouvard* too slow for consolation, and while on holiday at Concarneau in autumn 1875 turned to a totally different world, that of the Middle Ages, and a totally different scale, a short story rather than an epic treatment of human stupidity. By the following February (1876) the story of *Saint Julian* was completed, and the challenge of George Sand at once taken up. She had died in June 1876, before *A Simple Heart* was finished, but Flaubert, who had broken down at her funeral, did not falter in meeting her wishes beyond the grave. The impetus once generated, however painfully, carried him through to complete the third tale, *Herodias*, in three months, by early February 1877. Each tale appeared separately in serial form (between 12 and 27 February, with *A Simple Heart* coming first) before the three were published together on 24 April 1877 in the order here presented.

There is evidence that the speed of composition towards the end, and the decision to stop at three short stories before resuming work on *Bouvard*, were principally determined by Flaubert's urgent need for money and the publisher's calendar. With hindsight one can say, as most critics have done, that the three tales make up a balanced anthology in miniature of Flaubert's *œuvre*, but neither the number nor the content correspond to any overall scheme or unifying factor. Nevertheless the *Three Tales* afford a convenient and characteristic introduction to an author whose longer works may, even in translation, intimidate the reader hitherto familiar only with nineteenth-century authors of a more conventional kind.

One of the most obvious formal differences between the stories is that the first two trace the lives of Félicité and Julian from birth to death, while the whole action of the third takes place on Antipas' birthday, with a final page for the morning after. Again, the centrality of the main characters is basic to the first two stories, whereas the main speaking part, as it were, in *Herodias* goes to Antipas, even if the plot (in a literal sense) involving Salome on that particular day had been long since prepared by Herodias. There is moreover a deliberate ambiguity in the role allotted to Iaokanann: on the one hand the unfamiliar form of his name enables the reader to assess his importance without anachronistic preconceptions, on the other, the careful identification, at the first mention of that name, with Saint John the Baptist (let alone the concluding description of his head being borne away to Galilee where Jesus is) positively invites a Christian historical reading. What is perhaps more to the point is that all three stories build up to a death which alone gives proper perspective to all that has gone before. The official status of Julian and John is recalled from the start, but in each case a mysterious prediction of their end allows for very effective use of dramatic irony; only a few days after Julian's birth each of his parents is given an almost hallucinatory message concerning the child, which neither reveals to the other or to Julian, who in his turn, in adolescence, hears part of his future announced by the terrible stag, and each of them reacts inappropriately. Early on the fateful day Antipas too is told what lies written in the stars, but only understands the significance of the prediction when it is too late. As for Félicité, her end is not only private, since Mère Simon, though in the room, is looking out of the window at the crucial time, but unsuspected by any witness, then or later; for her apotheosis takes place in her mind—or more accurately in the simplicity of her heart. In a sense she too is a saint, albeit humble and unrecognized, but the three stories are no more *about* sanctity than about fate, determinism, or the divine will.

Religion is, however, an essential component of all three: the Holy Spirit, in the form of Loulou, greets Félicité in her dying vision, the leper, transformed into Christ himself, carries Julian up to heaven, John's death is explained in the concluding lines as the precondition for Jesus' glory. These are not sudden *coups de théâtre* to bring down the curtain: from attending catechism to building altars of repose with Virginie the practice of religion and a naïve faith are integral parts of Félicité's life; Julian too from childhood to death is shown to be intimately involved in religious practice and belief; and the whole person and presence of Iaokanann is religious and a reproach to the others. Here for once Flaubert is content to present religion in neutral terms, indeed he is almost benevolent in his portrayal compared to his usual treatment of priests, or of Emma's pious phase in *Madame Bovary*, let alone the description of the first communion (still to be written) of the eponymous heroes of *Bouvard*. For all that, it cannot be too strongly emphasized that religion in the three tales is a theme, like landscape, banquets, or antiquity, to be depicted with artistry but without personal commitment. The absence of mockery and anticlericalism may be welcome to some readers, but it was not in order to spare their feelings, still less because he shared them, that Flaubert treated the theme of religion as he did.

A statue of Saint Julian is known to have given Flaubert the idea of treating the legend, presumably in some form shorter than a novel, as early as 1846. By 1856 he had even sketched out a plan, but serious work did not begin until twenty years later. The final line of the tale refers to a stained-glass window, somewhat disingenuously suggesting that the transformation of the episodes there depicted into a story of great psychological depth and picturesque detail was achieved by a stroke of the writer's magic wand. The truth is rather different, but in no way detracts from Flaubert's artistic creation. In its barest essentials the legend explains how Julian, a man of noble birth, became a ferryman and then a saint, in fact patron of the boatmen and fishermen's guild in Rouen who paid for the window still to be seen in the cathedral there; this incongruous activity was a penance for killing his own parents by mistake. Literary sources begin with the thirteenth-century compilation of lives of the saints known as the Golden Legend, which Flaubert acknowledged (in correspondence), and a slightly later, much more detailed, Prose Tale (itself a version of a poem) freely paraphrased in the nineteenth century. It is this nineteenth-century reworking, rather than any mediaeval manuscript, which now seems to have been his main source.

The changes he made are more interesting for what they tell us about his artistic preferences than about his originality as such. Mediaeval versions already contained the prediction by a stag (or other hunted beast) that Julian would kill his parents which motivates his sudden disappearance from home. Flaubert completely alters the reader's preparation for the fatal deed by introducing a new hunting-scene immediately beforehand which gives him full scope for grotesque and sinister invention. The sickening slaughter of Julian's earlier expedition (culminating in the episode with the stag) is directly reversed, in that countless animals and birds come within range, all are attacked, but none is hit, and all in concert then pursue with mockery their erstwhile pursuer. It is Julian's wounded pride and frustrated blood-lust that explicitly drive him to fulfil the prediction from which he had fled, and for which he had abandoned hunting until that very night. As a consequential twist his wife becomes not merely the occasion of his crime, through her kindly act of putting his parents in her bed, but also morally responsible, since she had made light of his fears and recurrent nightmares and urged him to resume his deadly pastime. The fact that she did this in good faith, hoping thereby to make him happier, does not excuse her, and after the funeral she disappears from the story. As a result, Julian's isolation is total, and instead of following the legend in making husband and wife share the penance, and ultimate forgiveness, Flaubert concentrates on Julian, the only character who interests him. The climax, like that of the next story, has no witnesses, but is carefully orchestrated: the raging storm, the crossing of the river, the leper's demands for food, drink, and warmth lead on directly to his transformation and to Julian's ascent into heaven, which in the sources comes only after Julian and his wife have successfully passed the test of the leper's demands (and a leper, incidentally, who is revealed as an angel, not Christ himself). These powerful set-pieces are probably what the majority of readers will find most impressive, both for the sustained description and for the irresistible dramatic tension, and, of course, the one ends the causal chain inaugurated by the other. It is an open question whether either, or both, is true to the mediaeval spirit which created the original legend; the two episodes are integral parts of a new creation by Flaubert, who exploits a mediaeval legend in a nineteenth-century way, and in so doing produces a variation superior to the original literary statement of the theme.

This tale raises a question about authenticity which in one form or another recurs in all Flaubert's historical work, and, indeed, in the other works as well. After his encyclopaedic reading for *Salammbo*, Flaubert was most annoyed by criticism of his scholarly accuracy, which he defended with some vigour. Both for *Saint Julian* and *Herodias* he took immense pains, in reading and consulting experts, to accumulate facts about architecture, hunting, geography, history, and much else, which he then inserted into the tales; even for *A Simple Heart* he briefed himself on medical, liturgical, and ornithological details, and the stuffed parrot borrowed for his writing desk has become legendary. It is clear therefore that he wanted to immerse himself in this kind of detail, that it helped him

to write and that, however recondite, a source can be
assumed (and usually identified) for any given piece of
information. That said, it must be added that Flaubert was
manifestly not concerned with slavish (as he would have
seen it) submission to the facts. Anachronism of events in
Herodias is total, and in *Saint Julian*, which is based on
legend rather than history, anachronistic details of décor
rather than structure abound: for instance, Julian's mother
wears a hennin, a fifteenth-century fashion, in a thirteenth-
century legend. It could be argued that cavalier disregard
for accuracy is itself a feature of mediaeval literature, in
which, for example, Saracens are commonly represented as
idolaters, but that is to miss the point. After all, the *Three
Tales* were composed as a respite from *Bouvard*, for which
an unprecedented amount of reading enabled Flaubert to
denounce the futility of amassing erudition over the whole
range of arts and sciences. The only appropriate criterion
is aesthetic; it does not matter if facts are inconsistent, or
distorted by fiction, it does matter if their accumulation
begins to pall. What most strikes the reader as authentic is
atmosphere, not this or that detail.

A Simple Heart is in a very different category. There is no
literary model, and the events recounted belong to a past
sufficiently recent for living memory to replace recorded
history. All the places, most of the people and even some
of the incidents can be linked to elements of Flaubert's own
direct experience. His mother came from Pont-l'Évêque,
which he had known well, his aunt lived there, Trouville
was a favourite scene of family holidays, the death of Virginie
(and the childhood of Paul) recalls that of Flaubert's adored
only sister Caroline, who died not in adolescence but in
1846, giving birth at the age of twenty-two to his equally
adored niece Caroline. The first attack of his pseudo-epileptic
nervous illness (1844) actually occurred at the very spot on
the road where Félicité is knocked senseless by a blow from

the coachman's whip. As for the parrot, living and dead, there is no lack of models, and Julian Barnes's eponymous novel does full justice to that subject. It is highly significant that as well as taking the trouble to read about parrots, and to acquire one or more stuffed specimens, Flaubert felt the need to revisit Pont-l'Évêque and Honfleur, well known since his childhood and only a few miles from Croisset across the river, so that he could steep himself in the local atmosphere. In fact the effect of the visit was less informative regarding detail than poignant in arousing memories and emotions. At least twice in the story he slips into the present tense (in describing the farm at Geffosses and the convent garden at Honfleur), as if to emphasize that the passage of time has left some things unchanged. In theory almost the whole story could have been composed from a mosaic of personal memory and other people's local gossip, but even before the purely imaginary vision of the final page, some of the most memorable passages involve the private emotions of Félicité, alone, deaf, going blind, with only the parrot to console her—her untypical surrender to grief after the incident with the coach is a good example. Artistically the scene rings true, though it is wholly invented, in a way that accurate topography, for instance, does not. Sometimes, it must be admitted, even Flaubert nods, and Félicité's preposterous but successful race to catch up with the doctor's gig the night before Virginie dies, and her reluctant return when she realizes she has forgotten to lock up the house, jar artistically as much as the later coach episode convinces. Even with the extraneous knowledge that the story was written specifically to meet George Sand's challenge, the reader does not feel that mere literary skill is being used to disguise Flaubert's more characteristically negative emotions. Félicité is as different as could be from her creator, and yet elicits our sympathy through his remarkable empathy with her. The keynote is tenderness, not sentimentality.

As regards the source of *Herodias*, there is a mediaeval sculpture group in Rouen Cathedral showing Salome dancing upside down on her hands, and by analogy with the Julian window it has been suggested that Flaubert's initial choice of subject was triggered by this. However, the Gospels of Matthew and Mark, and innumerable legendary versions thereafter, have made the story so familiar that it seems pointless to look for a specific source of inspiration. On the other hand, Flaubert's treatment of the event was from the first intended to be independent of religious (and spiritual) implications, and thus for a politico-historical account of what happened he inevitably had recourse to Flavius Josephus, born a Jew, later enrolled as a Pharisee, who then went over to the Romans and served their cause. To the question 'what did people at the time, on the spot, think of John's execution and Jesus' ministry?' Flaubert is enabled to offer a reasonably plausible answer, but his attitude to historical accuracy, as distinct from atmosphere, is even more nonchalant than it had been in *Salammbo*. Virtually all the events, meetings, and positions held are anachronistic as mentioned, although they occur *somewhere* in the history of the relevant decades. It would be tedious to rehearse all the deliberate alterations made to Josephus' account, but what is interesting is that the story does follow the lines hinted at in Mark: John's imprisonment is ascribed to Herodias' anger at his denunciation of her marriage to Antipas while her first husband, Antipas' brother, is still alive; Antipas himself is stated to have respected John; his rash promise to grant Salome any wish, made in public at the birthday feast, is explicitly motivated by the effect on him of her dance, and the demand for John's head by the prompting of Herodias. Thus the family and emotional relationships of the main characters are portrayed in accordance with the best known source (and Mark is preferred to Matthew where they differ), but the background events are very liberally modified. In particular the presence of Vitellius and his repulsive son at the feast is completely unhistorical, but crucial to Flaubert's narrative and his dramatic presentation of the banquet, with its gruesome confrontation between Aulus and the severed head as dénouement. Topography, the site of Machaerus, the characteristics of the innumerable racial and religious groups tirelessly squabbling in the region, details of food and clothing, all are carefully recreated with a wealth of description, noise and colour anticipating that of the biblical epics to be produced in modern times for the cinema. By focusing on psychological truths Flaubert can achieve artistic authenticity while ignoring historical accuracy.

If there is a weakness in *Herodias*, it derives from the author's relentless determination to spare the reader no item of the information so painstakingly gleaned from research. The fasces of the lictors, the phylacteries of the pious Jews, the reason for the Samaritans' hatred of the Jews, the nature of clean and unclean foods, all is explained, catalogued, annotated. As in *Salammbo* the effect can eventually be self-defeating through sheer weight of fact.

A difficulty facing the translator, and, it seems, even the intelligent French reader, should be mentioned, though it would be rash to impute it as a weakness to an author so obsessively concerned with style as Flaubert. The ellipsis so characteristic of his narrative style undoubtedly conveys a sense of tension and immediacy, but in two respects it often leads to obscurity. Pronouns are habitually used in preference to proper names, and when *elle* or *il* is used three times in the same sentence, referring each time to a different person, the translator is obliged to supply a proper name for the sake of clarity. Again the constant use of *style indirect libre* to represent a more or less free version of a character's words or thoughts without the use of direct speech (in fact very rare in this work) leaves the reader in doubt as to how much was spoken, how much remained a fleeting but silent thought. Unlike the ambiguous use of pronouns, this particular obscurity cannot be satisfactorily dispelled, because there is no criterion, linguistic or contextual, by which to resolve it. It should not be necessary to add that in all great art, and not only in literature, facility of interpretation may be a convenience, but is far from being a necessary virtue. In this case fidelity to Flaubert has generally been preferred, even at the risk of obscurity, rather than the insertion of gratuitous 'he said', 'she thought', and the like.

A.J.K.

NOTE ON THE TEXT

THE text used for this translation follows that of the original edition of 1877 approved by Flaubert.

FURTHER READING

FOR those unfamiliar with Flaubert's work, the most obvious and useful further reading would be his principal novels: *Madame Bovary*, *Sentimental Education*, *Salammbô*, and *Bouvard and Pécuchet*, all of which can be found in one or more English translations.

For *Three Tales* there is surprisingly little, considering how popular the book has always been. Critical works on Flaubert either ignore the tales completely, or devote only a few pages to them. The most thorough treatment in English is the edition of the French text by Colin Duckworth (Harrap, London, 1959, subsequently reprinted). This has a full introduction and copious notes, a few only of which need correction. The main objection to this edition is that the source of *Saint Julian* has now been shown *not* to have been the mediaeval manuscript proposed by Duckworth; for a full discussion see B. J. Bart and R. F. Cook, *The Legendary Source of Flaubert's Saint Julian* (Toronto, 1977). In the usually excellent Grant and Cutler series 'Critical Guides to French Texts' one is promised by A. W. Raitt on *Flaubert: Trois Contes* in the near future. Finally, a book which is described as a novel, but really defies classification, is Julian Barnes, *Flaubert's Parrot* (London, 1984), a remarkably erudite, critical, perceptive, and original approach to the writer, using the bird in question as a focus, but going far beyond that specific problem.

A CHRONOLOGY OF
GUSTAVE FLAUBERT

1821   12 December: born in Rouen, where his father is chief surgeon at the Hôtel-Dieu.

1836   While at school in Rouen, writes several stories. On holiday at Trouville, falls in love with Elisa Foucault, a woman of twenty-six, who shortly afterwards marries Maurice Schlésinger. The image of Elisa Schlésinger recurs in a number of Flaubert's writings: in particular, she is said to be the model for Madame Arnoux in *L'Éducation sentimentale*.

1837   More stories. One of these, *Une leçon d'histoire naturelle, genre Commis*, is published in a local journal; another, *Passion et vertu*, anticipates the story of *Madame Bovary* in certain respects.

1838   *Mémoires d'un fou*, an autobiographical narrative; *Loys XI*, a five-act play.

1839   Completes *Smarh*, a semi-dramatic fantasy which may be considered an embryonic version of *La Tentation de Saint Antoine*.

1842   *Novembre*, another autobiographical narrative. Passes his first law examination.

1843   Begins the first version of *L'Éducation sentimentale*. Fails his second law examination.

1844   Has a form of epileptic seizure. Gives up law.

1845   *L'Éducation sentimentale* (first version) completed.

1846   Flaubert's father and sister die. He sets up house at Croisset, near Rouen, with his mother and niece. Meets Louise Colet in Paris; she becomes his mistress.

1847   *Par les champs et par les grèves*, impressions of his travels in Brittany with his literary friend Maxime Du Camp.

1848   Together with Louis Bouilhet (another literary friend) and Maxime Du Camp, witnesses the 1848 uprising in Paris; he will later draw on these memories for scenes in *L'Éducation sentimentale*. Begins *La Tentation de Saint Antoine* (first version).

1849   Reads *La Tentation* aloud to Bouilhet and Du Camp, who consider it a failure. Leaves for a tour of the Near East with Du Camp.

1851   Returns to Croisset. 19 September: begins writing *Madame Bovary*.

1852   While working on *Madame Bovary*, recalls his earlier project for a *Dictionnaire des idées reçues*.

1854   End of affair with Louise Colet.

1856   *Madame Bovary* completed and published in serial form in *La Revue de Paris* (from 1 October). Begins to revise *La Tentation*.

1856–7 Fragments of *La Tentation* published in *L'Artiste*.

1857   Flaubert and *La Revue de Paris* prosecuted for irreligion and immorality; acquitted. The trial attracts a great deal of attention and makes *Madame Bovary* (now published as a complete novel) a *succès de scandale*. Begins work on *Salammbô*.

1858   Visits North Africa to gather material for *Salammbô*.

1862   *Salammbô* completed and published: an enormous success. Flaubert by now a famous literary figure.

1864   Begins work on *L'Éducation sentimentale*. In the course of the next five years gathers material for his novel, and at the same time enjoys a brilliant social life.

1869   *L'Éducation sentimentale* (definitive version) completed and published. Death of Louis Bouilhet.

1870   Works on yet another version of *La Tentation de Saint Antoine*.

1872   Flaubert's mother dies. Third version of *La Tentation* completed.

1874 *La Tentation* published. Begins work on *Bouvard et Pécuchet*.

1875–7 Writes *La Légende de Saint Julien l'Hospitalier*, *Un coeur simple*, and *Hérodias* (*Trois Contes*).

1877 *Trois Contes* published. Returns to *Bouvard et Pécuchet*.

1877–80 Works on *Bouvard*, which will remain unfinished.

1880 8 May: dies.

1881 *Bouvard et Pécuchet* published.

THREE TALES

THREE TALES

A Simple Heart

FOR half a century the good ladies of Pont-l'Évêque envied Madame Aubain her servant Félicité.

For one hundred francs a year she did the cooking and the housework, sewing, washing, and ironing, she could bridle a horse, fatten up poultry, churn butter, and remained faithful to her mistress, who was not however a very likeable person.

She had married a handsome but impecunious young man, who died at the beginning of 1809, leaving her with two very young children and heavy debts. So she sold her properties, except the farms at Toucques and Geffosses, which brought in five thousand francs a year at the very most, and moved out of her house at Saint-Melaine into a less expensive one, which had been in her family for generations and stood behind the market-hall.

This house, faced with slates, lay between an alley and a lane running down to the river. Inside there were changes of level which could make you stumble. A narrow entrance hall separated the kitchen from the living-room, where Madame Aubain sat all day long in a basketwork armchair by the window. Against the white-painted panelling were ranged eight mahogany chairs. On an old piano, beneath a barometer, rested a pyramid of piled-up boxes and cartons. A tapestry wing-chair stood on each side of a yellow marble mantelpiece in Louis XV style. The clock in the middle of it represented a temple of Vesta—and the whole place smelled slightly of mildew, for the floor was lower than the garden.

On the first floor there came first 'Madame's' bedroom, very large, papered in a pale floral pattern, and containing a portrait of 'Monsieur' dressed as a dandy of days gone by.

This led into a smaller room, in which were two children's cots without mattresses. Then came the drawing-room, always kept shut up, and full of furniture covered in dust-sheets. Next, a corridor led to a study; books and papers filled the shelves of a bookcase whose three sides surrounded a large black wooden desk. The two corner panels were lost to view beneath pen-and-ink drawings, gouache landscapes, and Audran* prints, relics of better days and vanished luxury. A skylight on the second floor provided light for Félicité's room, which looked out over the meadows.

She would get up at dawn, so as not to miss Mass, and work without a break until evening; then, with dinner over, the dishes put away and the door securely locked, she would pile ashes over the log and doze in front of the hearth, her rosary in her hand. When it came to haggling no one was more persistent. As for cleanliness, her gleaming pots and pans were the despair of the other servants. Very thrifty, she ate slowly, and with her finger gathered up all the crumbs left on the table from her loaf of bread—a twelve-pound loaf, baked specially for her, which lasted three weeks.

Year in, year out, she wore a calico print neckerchief, fastened at the back with a pin, a bonnet which covered her hair, grey stockings, a red skirt, and over her jacket an apron with a bib, such as nurses wear in hospitals.

She had a thin face and a sharp voice. At twenty-five she was taken for forty. Once past fifty she could have been any age; and with her perpetual silence, straight back, and deliberate gestures she looked like a wooden dummy, driven by clockwork.

II

SHE had had, like anyone else, her love story.

Her father, a mason, had been killed falling off scaffolding. Then her mother died, her sisters scattered, a farmer took her in and while she was still a child employed her as cowherd in the open fields. She shivered with cold in her rags, lay flat to drink water out of the ponds, was beaten for no reason at all, and was finally thrown out for the theft of thirty sous,* which she had never stolen. She went to another farm, was put in charge of the poultry, and as the owners liked her the other farmhands were jealous.

One evening in August (she was then eighteen) they took her with them to the village fair at Colleville. Straight away she was dazed, deafened by the noise of the fiddles, the lights in the trees, the medley of brightly coloured costumes, lace, gold crosses, this mass of people all hopping about in time. She was standing shyly to one side when a prosperous-looking young man, who had been smoking a pipe as he leaned with both arms on a cart-shaft, came up and invited her to dance. He bought her cider, coffee, cake, a silk scarf, and imagining that she had guessed his intentions, offered to see her home. On the edge of a field of oats he brutally tumbled her over. She was frightened and began to scream. He made off.

Another evening, on the Beaumont road, she tried to get past a large haywain which was travelling slowly in front of her, and, brushing by close to the wheels, she recognized Théodore.

He greeted her quite calmly, saying that she must forgive his behaviour, since it was all 'the fault of the drink'.

She did not know how to reply, and wanted to run away.

At once he began talking about the crops and the leading figures of the commune, for his father had left Colleville for the farm at Les Écots, so that they were now neighbours. 'Ah!' she said. He added that his people wanted him to settle down, but he was in no hurry, and was waiting for a wife who would suit him. She bowed her head. Then he asked if she was thinking of getting married. She replied with a smile that it was wrong to make fun of people. 'But I'm not, I swear!' and he put his left arm round her waist; she walked on supported by his embrace; they slowed down. There was a soft breeze, the stars were shining, the huge load of hay swayed in front of them; and the four horses kicked up the dust as they plodded on. Then, unbidden, they turned off to the right. He kissed her again. She vanished into the darkness.

The following week Théodore persuaded her to agree to several assignations.

They would meet in some corner of a farmyard, behind a wall, under some isolated tree. She was not innocent in the way that young ladies are—she had learned from the animals—but her reason and innate sense of honour kept her from losing her virtue. Her resistance sharpened Théodore's desire, so that in the hope of satisfying it (or perhaps out of sheer naïvety) he proposed marriage to her. She was unready to believe him. He swore solemnly that he meant it.

Soon he had a matter of some concern to confess: his parents, the year before, had bought a substitute* to do his military service; but he was liable at any time to be called up again; the idea of serving in the Forces appalled him. Such cowardice was for Félicité proof of his affection; it made hers all the stronger. She would slip out at night to meet him, and once she arrived, Théodore would torment her with his worries and his pleas.

Finally he announced that he was going to the Prefecture himself to make enquiries, and would report the result the following Sunday night between eleven and midnight.

At the appointed time she hastened to her lover.

In his place she found one of his friends.

From him she learned that she was never to see Théodore again. In order to be exempt from conscription Théodore had married a very wealthy old woman, Madame Lehoussais of Toucques.

Her grief was uncontrollable. She flung herself on the ground, screamed, called on God and stayed moaning all alone in the fields until sunrise. Then she returned to the farm, announced her intention of leaving, and at the end of the month was paid off; with all her meagre possessions wrapped in a kerchief she made her way to Pont-l'Évêque.

In front of the inn she asked some questions of a lady in a widow's hood, who was in fact just looking for a cook. The girl did not know much, but seemed to be so willing and modest in her demands that Madame Aubain finally said:

'Very well, I will take you!'

A quarter of an hour later Félicité was installed in her house.

At first she lived there in a state of fear and trembling brought on by 'the kind of house' it was and the memory of 'Monsieur' hanging over everything! Paul and Virginie,* the former aged seven, the latter barely four, seemed to her to be made out of some precious material; she would give them rides on her back like a horse, and Madame Aubain told her to stop kissing them all the time, which hurt her deeply. However she was happy there. In such an agreeable environment her gloom had faded away.

Every Thursday the same regular visitors came to play a game of boston.* Félicité prepared the cards and footwarmers in advance. They arrived punctually at eight o'clock and left before it struck eleven.

Every Monday morning the secondhand dealer who lived down the lane would spread out on the ground his bits and pieces. Then the town would resound with the buzz of voices, mingled with horses neighing, lambs bleating, pigs grunting and carts clattering through the streets. Towards noon, when the market was at its height, a tall, old peasant, with a hooked nose and his cap on the back of his head, would appear on the doorstep: it was Robelin, who farmed Geffosses. Shortly afterwards came Liébard, who farmed at Toucques, short, red-faced, stout, wearing a grey jacket and leggings fitted with spurs.

They both offered their landlady chickens or cheese for sale. Wily as they were, Félicité invariably got the better of them, and they would go off filled with respect for her.

At irregular intervals Madame Aubain would receive a visit from the Marquis de Grémanville, an uncle of hers, ruined by debauch, who lived at Falaise on the last remnant of his land. He always arrived at lunchtime, with a dreadful poodle which soiled all the furniture with its paws. Despite his efforts to act the nobleman, going so far as to raise his hat every time he said: 'My late father', yielding to force of habit he would pour himself one drink after another, and come out with ribald remarks. Félicité would politely push him out: 'You have had enough, Monsieur de Grémanville! Some other time!' And would close the door on him.

It was a pleasure for her to open it to Monsieur Bourais, a former solicitor. His white tie and bald head, his frilled shirt-front, his ample brown frock-coat, the way he curved his arm when he took a pinch of snuff, his whole person affected her with that agitation which the spectacle of exceptional men commonly provokes.

As he managed 'Madame's' properties, he would shut himself up with her for hours in 'Monsieur's' study; he was always afraid of compromising himself, had boundless respect for the judiciary and some pretensions to knowledge of Latin.

As a way of combining instruction with pleasure, he gave the children an illustrated geography-book. The pictures represented scenes from different parts of the world, canni-bals with feather headdresses, an ape abducting a young lady, bedouins in the desert, a whale being harpooned, etc.

Paul would explain these engravings to Félicité. This was indeed the only literary education she ever had.

That of the children was provided by Guyot, a poor devil employed at the Town Hall, famous for his fine handwriting, who used to sharpen his penknife on his boot.

When the weather was fine they would set out early for the farm at Geffosses.

The farmyard lies on a slope, with the house in the middle, and the sea appears in the distance as a patch of grey.

Félicité would take slices of cold meat out of her bag, and they would eat their lunch in a room connecting with the dairy. It was all that remained of a country house no longer to be seen. The tattered wallpaper stirred with every draught. Madame Aubain would bow her head, overwhelmed with memories; and the children did not dare to go on talking. 'Do go and play!' she would say; they made themselves scarce.

Paul would go into the barn, catch birds, play ducks and drakes on the pond, or bang a stick against the massive casks, which were as resonant as drums.

Virginie fed the rabbits, or rushed off to pick cornflowers, running so fast that her little embroidered knickers showed.

One autumn evening they went back through the fields.

The moon in its first quarter lit up part of the sky, and mist floated like a scarf over the winding river Toucques. Cattle lying in the middle of the grass looked peaceably at these four people going past. In the third meadow some of them stood up, then formed a circle in front of them. 'Don't be afraid!' said Félicité, and keening softly she stroked the back of the nearest animal; it turned about, the others followed suit. But when they began to cross the next field a fearsome bellowing rent the air. It was a bull, hidden in the mist. It advanced on the two women. Madame Aubain was about to run. 'No! no! not so fast!' They walked more rapidly all the same, and could hear behind them the sound of heavy breathing coming closer. Hooves thudded like hammerblows on the grass; now it was charging at a gallop! Félicité turned round, and with both hands took up clods of earth which she threw into the bull's eyes. It lowered its muzzle, tossed its horns and was shaking with rage as it bellowed horribly. Madame Aubain, at the end of the field with the two children, was frantically looking for some way to get over the high bank. Félicité kept retreating in front of the bull, continually hurling clumps of turf which blinded it, crying all the while: 'Hurry! Hurry!'

Madame Aubain went down into the ditch, pushed Virginie, then Paul, up the bank and fell several times trying to climb it herself, before she finally succeeded after strenuous efforts.

The bull had backed Félicité up against a barred gate; it was slavering close enough to spatter her face, another second and it would gore her. She just had time to slip between two of the bars, and the great beast stopped in its tracks in amazement.

This event was talked about for many years at Pont-l'Évêque. Félicité took no pride in it, and had no idea that she had done anything heroic.

She was exclusively concerned with Virginie, who had developed a nervous ailment as a result of this fright; Monsieur Poupart, the doctor, advised sea-bathing at Trouville.

In those days not many people went there. Madame Aubain made enquiries, consulted Bourais, and made preparations as though for a long journey.

Her luggage went off the day before, in Liébard's cart. Next day he brought along two horses, one of which had a woman's saddle, with a velvet back-rest; and on the crupper of the other a rolled-up cloak formed a seat of sorts, on which Madame Aubain rode, sitting behind him. Félicité took charge of Virginie, and Paul mounted Monsieur Lechaptois's donkey, which he had lent on condition that they took great care of it.

The road was so bad that the eight kilometres took them two hours. The horses sank up to their pasterns in mud, and worked free by jerking their hindquarters; or else they stumbled against the ruts; at other times they had to jump. Liébard's mare would suddenly stop at certain points. He would wait patiently for her to go on again, and talk about the people whose property lay beside the road, adding moral reflections to his account of them. Thus in the middle of Toucques, as they passed beneath windows wreathed in nasturtiums, he said with a shrug of his shoulders: 'That's where a certain Madame Lehoussais lives. Instead of taking a young man . . .'. Félicité did not hear the rest; the horses were trotting, the donkey galloping; then they all turned on to a path, a gate opened, two lads appeared, and they dismounted by the cesspool, just in front of the door.

Mère Liébard effusively expressed her delight at the sight of her mistress. She served up a meal consisting of a sirloin, tripe, black pudding, fricassee of chicken, sparkling cider, a fruit tart and plums in brandy, accompanied by compliments to Madame, who was looking much better, Mademoiselle, who had become 'simply gorgeous', young Monsieur Paul, who had 'filled out' wonderfully, without forgetting their deceased grandparents, whom the Liébards had known, having been in the family's service for several generations. The farm, like them, looked somewhat antique. The ceiling beams were worm-eaten, the walls black with smoke, the window-panes grey with dust. An oak dresser held all kinds of utensils, pitchers, plates, pewter bowls, wolf-traps, sheep-shears; an enormous syringe amused the children. There was not one tree in the three yards without fungus growing at its foot or a clump of mistletoe in its branches. The wind had brought down a lot of them. They had started growing again from the middle; and they all bent under the weight of their apples. The thatched roofs, like brown velvet of uneven thickness, stood up to the fiercest gusts. The cart-shed, however, was falling down. Madame Aubain said that she would see to it, and gave the order to harness the animals again.

It took a further half-hour to reach Trouville. The little caravan had to dismount to pass by the Écores,* a cliff overhanging the boats below, and three minutes later, at the end of the quayside, they went into the courtyard of the Golden Lamb, kept by Mère David.*

Virginie after the first few days did not feel so weak, as a result of the change of air and sea-bathing. She bathed in her chemise, since she did not have a costume; and her maid dressed her afterwards in a Customs hut used by the bathers.

In the afternoons they went off with the donkey beyond the Roches-Noires, in the direction of Hennequeville. At first the path led up through undulating ground like the lawns in a park, then came out on to a plateau where pasture and ploughland alternated. By the wayside, holly bushes grew up out of bramble thickets; here and there a tall dead tree traced against the blue sky the zigzag pattern of its branches.

They almost always rested in a meadow, with Deauville on the left, Le Havre on the right and the open sea facing them. It sparkled in the sunshine, smooth as a mirror, so calm that one could barely hear the murmur of the waves; sparrows chirped out of sight, and the immense vault of the heavens arched over everything. Madame Aubain sat doing her needlework; Virginie beside her plaited rushes; Félicité picked lavender flowers; Paul was just bored and wanted to move on.

At other times they crossed the Toucques in a boat and went looking for seashells. Low tide uncovered sea-urchins, scallops, called locally 'godefiches',* jellyfish; and the children would run to catch the bubbles of foam blown away by the wind. As the waves broke sleepily on the sand, they rippled out along the shore, which stretched as far as the eye could see, but on the landward side was bounded by the dunes separating it from the Marais, a wide meadow shaped like a racecourse. When they came back that way, Trouville on the hillside in the background grew larger with every step, and with all its varied houses seemed to be blooming in cheerful disarray.

On days when it was too hot they never left their room. The dazzling brightness from outside interposed bars of light between the slats of the drawn blinds. Not a sound came from the village. Below, on the pavement, not a soul. Such widespread silence increased the general impression of tranquillity. In the distance caulkers hammered away at the hulls, and the smell of tar was borne on the sultry breeze.

The main entertainment was provided by the fishing boats coming in. As soon as they had passed the marker buoys, they began to tack. Their sails were lowered two-thirds of the way down the masts; and with the foresail bellying out like a balloon, they slid forward with waves lapping their sides to the middle of the harbour, where they suddenly dropped anchor. Then each boat took its place at the quayside. The sailors threw the squirming fish ashore, where a line of carts waited, and women in cotton bonnets reached forward to take the baskets and embrace their menfolk.

One day one of these women approached Félicité, who shortly afterwards came into the room quite overjoyed. She had found one of her sisters; and Nastasie Barette, whose married name was Leroux, appeared, clutching a baby to her breast, another child in her right hand, and on her left a little ship's boy, with hands on hips and beret cocked over one ear.

After quarter of an hour Madame Aubain sent her off.

They kept coming across them, outside the kitchen, or when they went out for walks. The husband did not make an appearance.

Félicité became very fond of them. She bought them a blanket, some shirts, a stove; they were obviously exploiting her. This weakness annoyed Madame Aubain; besides she did not like the familiar way in which the nephew addressed her son, and as Virginie had developed a cough and the best of the season was over, she returned to Pont-l'Évêque.

Monsieur Bourais advised her on the choice of a school. The one at Caen was considered to be the best. Paul was sent there, and bravely said goodbye to everyone, pleased that he was going to live somewhere where he would have other boys to keep him company.

Madame Aubain resigned herself to her son's departure, because it had to be. Virginie thought about him less and less. Félicité missed the noise he used to make. But something else came up to keep her busy and distract her; starting at Christmas she took the little girl to catechism every day.

III

AFTER genuflecting at the door, she would walk between the double row of chairs beneath the lofty vault of the nave, open Madame Aubain's pew, sit down and look around.

The choir stalls were filled with boys on the right, girls on the left; the curé stood by the lectern; one stained-glass window in the apse depicted the Holy Spirit above the Virgin; another showed her kneeling before the infant Jesus, and behind the tabernacle a wooden carving represented Saint Michael slaying the dragon.

The priest began with a summary of Sacred History. In her mind's eye she saw Paradise, the Flood, the Tower of Babel, the cities destroyed by fire, whole peoples dying, idols overthrown; and this dazzling vision left her with lasting respect for the Almighty and fear of his wrath. Then she wept as she listened to the story of the Passion. Why had they crucified him, he who loved children, fed the multitude, healed the blind, and had been willing, in his meekness, to be born among the poor, in the muck of a stable? Sowing, harvesting, pressing, all these familiar things of which the Gospel speaks were part of her life; God had sanctified them with his passing presence; and she loved lambs more dearly from love of the Lamb of God, doves because of the Holy Spirit.

She found it hard to visualize what he looked like, for he was not just a bird, but a fire as well, and at other times a breath. Perhaps it was his light fluttering at night on the edge of the marshes, his breath driving the clouds, his voice making the bells ring tunefully; and she sat lost in worship, enjoying the coolness of the walls and the peaceful church.

As for dogma, she did not understand, did not even attempt to understand, a word of it. The curé would say his piece, the children would repeat it, she would eventually doze off; and would wake with a start at the noise of their sabots clattering down the stone paving on their way out.

This was how she learned the catechism, from hearing it repeated, for her religious education had been neglected in her youth; and as for practice, from that time on she simply copied Virginie, fasting like her, going to confession with her. At Corpus Christi they made an altar of repose* together.

The First Communion worried her a great deal beforehand. She fussed about the shoes, the rosary, the prayer book, the gloves. How she trembled as she helped Virginie's mother dress her!

All through the Mass she was on tenterhooks. Monsieur Bourais blocked her view of one side of the choir; but directly opposite her the band of maidens with their white wreaths worn over their lowered veils looked like a snowfield; and she recognized the precious child even at a distance by her slender neck and devout bearing. The bell tinkled. Heads were bowed; there was silence. As the organ thundered out choir and congregation intoned the Agnus Dei; then the boys began to file up, and after them the girls stood up. In slow procession, hands folded, they went up to the brightly lit altar, knelt on the first step, received the host in turn, and in the same order returned to their stalls. When it came to Virginie's turn, Félicité leaned forward to see her; and imagining things as one can when moved by genuine affection, it seemed to her that she herself was that child; the child's face became her own, she wore the child's dress, the child's heart beat in her breast; when the moment came to open her mouth and close her eyes Félicité all but fainted.

Early next morning she went to the sacristy and asked Monsieur le curé to give her communion. She received it most devoutly, but without the ecstasy she had experienced the day before.

Madame Aubain wanted her daughter to be endowed with every accomplishment; and as Guyot was unable to teach her English or music, she decided to send her as a boarder to the Ursulines at Honfleur.

The child raised no objections. Félicité sighed, finding Madame heartless. Then she reflected that her mistress might be right. Such matters were beyond her capacities.

Finally one day an old break drew up at the door; and out stepped a nun who had come to fetch Mademoiselle. Félicité hauled the luggage up on the roof, gave the coachman instructions, and stowed in the boot six pots of jam and a dozen pears, with a bouquet of violets.

At the last moment Virginie was overcome by a fit of sobbing; she hugged her mother, who kissed her on the forehead, repeating: 'Come now! be brave! be brave!' The step was raised and the break moved off.

Then Madame Aubain collapsed; and that evening all her friends, the Lormeaus, Madame Lechaptois, *those** Mesdemoiselles Rochefeuille, Monsieur de Houppeville, and Bourais came round to console her.

At first she found it extremely painful to be without her daughter. But three times a week she had a letter from her, and on the other days wrote back. She walked in her garden, read a little, and in this way filled the empty hours.

In the morning, from force of habit, Félicité would go into Virginie's room, and look round the four walls. She missed having to comb the girl's hair, lace up her boots, tuck her up in bed—and constantly seeing her sweet face, holding her hand when they went out together. With nothing else to do she tried her hand at lace-making. Her clumsy fingers broke the threads; she could not concentrate, was losing sleep, in her own words was 'undermined'.

'To take her mind off it' she asked if she might be allowed to receive visits from her nephew Victor.

He would arrive on Sundays after Mass, rosy-cheeked, bare-chested and smelling of the countryside he had come through. She would straight away lay a place for him. They would have their lunch facing each other; and though she herself ate as little as possible to save expense, she would fill him up with so much food that he would end by falling asleep. As soon as the bell began to ring for Vespers she roused him, brushed his trousers, tied his tie and made her way to church, leaning on his arm with maternal pride.

His parents always told him to get something out of her, a packet of brown sugar, perhaps, or some soap, brandy, sometimes even money. He would bring her his clothes to mend; and she was happy to accept the task, because it meant that he would have to come back.

In August his father took him on voyages round the coast.

It was the time of the school holidays. The children's arrival consoled her. But Paul was becoming capricious, and Virginie was now too old to be spoken to familiarly as a child; that caused a certain constraint, set up a barrier between them.

Victor went successively to Morlaix, Dunkirk, and Brighton; he brought her back a present from each voyage. The first time it was a box decorated with seashells; the second time a coffee cup; the third time a big gingerbread man. He was turning out a handsome lad, with his slim waist, a faint moustache, a good honest look and a little leather cap, worn on the back of his head, like a pilot. He entertained her by telling stories mixed up with nautical language.

One Monday, the fourteenth of July 1819 (she never forgot the date) Victor announced that he had signed on for an ocean voyage, and on the Wednesday night would be taking the packet-boat from Honfleur to join his schooner, which was due to sail shortly from Le Havre. He might be away for as much as two years.

The prospect of such a long absence grieved Félicité deeply, and wanting to bid him another farewell, on the Wednesday evening, after Madame's dinner, she put on her clogs and made short work of the four leagues* between Pont-l'Évêque and Honfleur.

When she reached the Calvary, instead of bearing left, she bore right, got lost in the shipyards, retraced her steps; some people she approached urged her to hurry. She went all round the docks, which were full of shipping, stumbling over mooring ropes; then the level of the ground fell, there were beams of light criss-crossing in all directions, and she thought she was going mad when she saw some horses up in the air.

On the quayside others were whinnying, frightened by the sea. A hoist was lifting them up and lowering them into a boat, where passengers jostled among casks of cider, baskets of cheese, sacks of grain; hens were clucking, the captain swearing; and a cabin boy was leaning on the cathead, quite indifferent to everything. Félicité, who had not recognized him, cried 'Victor!' repeatedly, and he looked up; she rushed forward, but the gangway was suddenly pulled in.

The packet-boat, hauled by women singing as they went, left harbour. Its ribs creaked, heavy waves lashed its bows. The sail had swung round, there was no longer anyone to be seen; and against the sea shining silver in the moonlight it stood out as a dark patch, which steadily faded, sank away, disappeared.

As Félicité went past the Calvary she wanted to commend to God all that she held most dear; and she stood praying for a long time, her face wet with tears, her eyes lifted up to the clouds. The town slept, Customs men did their rounds; and water poured incessantly through the holes in the lockgate, sounding like a torrent. It struck two.

The convent parlour* would not be open before daylight. If she were late back Madame would certainly be annoyed; and despite her desire to embrace the other child, she started home. The girls in the inn were just waking up as she came into Pont-l'Évêque.

So the poor lad would be rolling about on the ocean waves for months on end! His earlier voyages had not alarmed her. People came back from England and Brittany; but America, the Colonies, the Islands,* that was away in some remote, vague region at the other end of the world.

From that moment Félicité's only thoughts were for her nephew. On sunny days she worried about his thirst; when there was a thunderstorm she was afraid that he would be struck by lightning. As she listened to the wind howling in the chimney and blowing off roof slates, she saw him battered by the same gale, on the top of some shattered mast, his whole body bent back beneath a blanket of foam; or else, as she remembered the geography picture-book, he was being eaten by savages, caught in a forest by apes, perishing on some deserted shore. And she never talked about her worries.

Madame Aubain had her own worries, concerning her daughter.

The nuns found her affectionate, but delicate. The slightest excitement tired her out. She had to give up the piano.

Her mother insisted on regular letters from the convent. One morning when the postman had not called she grew impatient; and paced up and down the room, from her chair to the window. It was quite extraordinary! four days now without news!

Trying to console her with her own example, Félicité said to her:

'But Madame, I haven't had any for six months!'

'From whom . . .?'

The servant quietly replied:

'Why, from my nephew!'

'Oh! your nephew!' And shrugging her shoulders Madame Aubain resumed her pacing, which meant: 'I never thought of him! . . . Besides, what do I care! A worthless cabin boy, of no account! . . . Whereas my daughter . . . Just imagine!'

Félicité, though brought up the hard way, was angry with Madame, then forgot about it.

It seemed so easy to her to lose one's head on account of the little girl.

The two children were of equal importance to her; they were united by the bond in her heart, and their destiny should be the same.

She learned from the pharmacist that Victor's boat had arrived in Havana. He had read the information in a newspaper.

Because of the cigars she imagined Havana as a place where nobody did anything but smoke, and she saw Victor walking about among negroes in a cloud of tobacco smoke. 'In case of need' could one come back overland? How far was it from Pont-l'Évêque? To find out she asked Monsieur Bourais.

He got out his atlas and began to explain all about longitudes; and put on a pedantically superior smile at Félicité's bewilderment. At length he pointed with his pencil at an imperceptible black dot somewhere in the indentations of an oval patch,* adding: 'There it is.' She bent over the map; the network of coloured lines tired her eyes without making her any the wiser; and when Bourais asked what was bothering her, she begged him to show her the house where Victor was living. Bourais flung up his arms, sneezed, laughed uproariously, revelling in such ingenuousness; and Félicité could not understand why—her intelligence was so limited that she might even be expecting to see her nephew's portrait!

It was a fortnight later that Liébard came as usual into the kitchen at market time, and handed her a letter sent by her brother-in-law. As neither of them could read, she had recourse to her mistress.

Madame Aubain, who was counting the stitches in her knitting, laid it aside, opened the letter, gave a start, and looking intently at her said in a low voice:

'They are writing to give you some . . . bad news. Your nephew . . .'

He was dead. There were no further details.

Félicité fell on to a chair, rested her head against the wall, and closed her eyelids, which suddenly reddened. Then with head bowed, hands dangling, fixed stare, she repeated time after time:

'Poor young lad! poor young lad!'

Liébard sighed as he watched her. Madame Aubain was trembling slightly.

She suggested that Félicité should go and see her sister at Trouville.

Félicité made a gesture to indicate that there was no need.

There was a silence. Liébard decided that he ought to leave.

Then she said:

'Them! It means nothing to them!'

Her head drooped again; and from time to time without thinking she picked up the long knitting-needles from the work table.

Some women went by in the yard carrying some laundry, still dripping, on a kind of stretcher.

Seeing them through the window reminded her of her own washing; she had boiled it up the day before, so today she had to rinse it; and she left the room.

Her washboard and tub lay beside the Toucques. She threw a pile of shifts down on the river bank, rolled up her sleeves, picked up her beater, and pounded so hard with it that the sound could be heard in the adjoining gardens. The meadows were empty, the wind ruffled the river; on the bottom long weeds streamed out like the hair of corpses floating in the water. She held back her grief, and was very brave until the evening; but in her bedroom she gave way to it, lying prone on the mattress, face pressed into the pillow, fists clenched against her temples.

Much later she heard from Victor's captain himself the circumstances of his death. He had been taken to hospital with yellow fever, and they had bled him too much. Four doctors had held him at once. He had died immediately, and the head one had said:

'Right! one more . . .!'

His parents had always treated him with inhumanity. She preferred not to see them again; and they made no advances, either from forgetfulness or the callousness of the poor.

Virginie was growing weaker.

Frequent difficulty in breathing, coughing, continual fever and blotches on her cheeks indicated some deep-seated ailment. Monsieur Poupart had advised a stay in Provence. Madame Aubain decided on that, and would have brought her daughter straight home, but for the climate of Pont-L'Évêque.

She came to an arrangement with a man who hired out carriages, and he took her to the convent every Tuesday. In the garden is a terrace with a view of the Seine. Virginie would walk there, on her arm, treading on fallen vine-leaves. Sometimes the sun coming through the clouds made her blink as she looked at sails in the distance and the whole horizon, from the castle at Tancarville round to the lighthouses of Le Havre. Then they would have a rest beneath the arbour. Her mother had obtained a small cask of excellent Malaga wine; and laughing at the idea of getting tipsy, Virginie would take two sips, never more.

Her strength began to return. The autumn passed by quietly. Félicité spoke reassuringly to Madame Aubain. But one evening when she had been out on some errand nearby, she came upon Monsieur Poupart's cabriolet in front of the door, and he was in the hall. Madame Aubain was fastening her hat.

'Give me my footwarmer, my purse, my gloves; do hurry up!'

Virginie had pleurisy; it might be hopeless.

'Not yet!' said the doctor; and they both got into the gig, with snowflakes swirling down. It would soon be dark. It was very cold.

Félicité rushed to the church to light a candle. Then she ran after the gig, caught up with it an hour later, nimbly jumped on behind, and was clinging to the fringed hood when she suddenly thought: 'The courtyard was never locked up! What if thieves broke in?' And she jumped down.

Next day, at first light, she went round to the doctor's house. He had returned, and gone off again on his country rounds. Then she waited at the inn, thinking that was where strangers would bring a letter. Finally, as dusk fell, she took the coach coming from Lisieux.

The convent lay at the end of a steep lane. About halfway down she heard a strange sound, the tolling of a death-knell. 'It's for someone else,' she thought; and Félicité banged the door knocker violently.

After several minutes she heard slippers shuffling along. The door opened a crack and a nun appeared.

The good sister said sorrowfully that 'she had just passed away'. At the same moment the tolling from Saint-Léonard's grew louder.

Félicité reached the second floor.

From the doorway of the room she could see Virginie lying on her back, with hands folded, mouth open, and head thrown back beneath a black crucifix which leaned towards her, her face still paler than the curtains hanging motionless on either side. Madame Aubain was clinging to the foot of the bed, choking with sobs of anguish. The Mother Superior stood on the right. Three candlesticks on the chest of drawers added splashes of red, and the fog was turning the windows white. Nuns led Madame Aubain away.

For two whole nights Félicité never left the dead girl. She kept repeating the same prayers, sprinkling holy water over the sheets, sitting down again, gazing at her. At the end of the first vigil she noticed that the face had turned yellow, the lips blue, the nose was becoming pinched, the eyes more sunken. She kissed the eyes several times; and would not have been vastly astonished if Virginie had opened them; for such souls the supernatural is quite simple. She laid out the corpse, wrapped it in the shroud, lowered it into the coffin, put on a wreath, spread out the hair. It was fair hair, exceptionally long for her age. Félicité cut off a large lock, and slipped half of it into her bosom, determined never to let it go.

The body was brought back to Pont-l'Évêque, in accordance with the wishes of Madame Aubain, who followed the hearse in a closed carriage.

After the Mass it took another three-quarters of an hour to reach the cemetery. Paul walked in front, sobbing. Monsieur Bourais came behind him, then the leading townsfolk, the women in long black veils, and Félicité. She was thinking of her nephew, to whom she had been unable to pay these last respects, and this added to her sorrow, as if he were being buried with the other child.

Madame Aubain's despair knew no bounds.

First she rebelled against God, whom she looked on as unjust for taking away her daughter—she had never done anything wrong, her conscience was so clear! But no! She should have taken her to the South of France. Other doctors would have saved her! She blamed herself, wanted to join her daughter, cried out in distress in the middle of her dreams. One dream in particular obsessed her. Her husband, dressed as a sailor, was returning from a long voyage, and told her with tears that he had been ordered to take Virginie away. Then they would put their heads together to discover some safe hiding-place.

Once she came in from the garden quite distraught. A moment before (she showed the exact spot) father and daughter had appeared to her side by side; they were not doing anything; they just looked at her.

For several months she stayed in her room in a state of apathy. Félicité gently chided her; she must look after herself for her son's sake, and for her husband's, in memory of 'her'.

'Her?' replied Madame Aubain, as if waking from sleep. 'Oh! yes! yes! . . . You are not forgetting her!' Referring to the cemetery, where she had been strictly forbidden to go.

Félicité went there every day.

Punctually at four o'clock she skirted the houses, went up the hill, opened the gate and came to Virginie's grave. It consisted of a small pink marble column, with a tombstone at the bottom, surrounded by chains enclosing a little garden plot. The beds were completely covered over with flowers. She would water their leaves, put down fresh sand, go down on her knees to dig the ground more thoroughly. When Madame Aubain was finally able to go there, she felt relieved, somehow comforted, by this.

Then years went by, all alike and without incident, apart from the great festivals as they came round: Easter,

Assumption, All Saints. Domestic events marked a date, subsequently used as a point of reference. Thus in 1825 two glaziers whitewashed the hall; in 1827 part of the roof fell into the courtyard and narrowly missed killing a man. In the summer of 1828 it was Madame's turn to present the blessed bread;* at about that time Bourais went mysteriously absent; and old acquaintances gradually departed: Guyot, Liébard, Madame Lechaptois, Robelin, uncle Grémanville, who had been paralysed for years.

One night the driver of the mail-coach brought Pont-l'Évêque the news of the July Revolution.* A new sub-prefect was appointed a few days later: Baron de Larsonnière, a former consul in America, whose household included, apart from his wife, his sister-in-law with three young ladies, already quite grown-up. They could be seen on their lawn, dressed in loose smocks; they owned a negro and a parrot. Madame Aubain received a formal call from them, and did not fail to return it. At the first glimpse of them in the distance Félicité would run to warn her. But only one thing could arouse her feelings; her son's letters.

He could not follow any career, because he spent all his time in taverns. She paid his debts, he contracted new ones; and as Madame Aubain sat knitting at the window she would sigh loudly enough for Félicité to hear as she turned her spinning-wheel in the kitchen.

They would stroll together beside the espalier, and always talked about Virginie, discussing whether she would have liked this or that, or what she would probably have said on such and such an occasion.

All her modest belongings filled a cupboard in the children's bedroom. Madame Aubain inspected them as seldom as possible. One summer's day she resigned herself to do so; and moths flew out of the wardrobe.

Her dresses hung in a row under a shelf containing three dolls, some hoops, a set of doll's furniture, and the wash-basin she had used. They also took out petticoats, stockings, handkerchiefs, and spread them out on the two beds before folding them up again. The sun shone brightly on these shabby things, showing up the stains, and creases caused by movements of her body. The air was warm, the sky blue, a blackbird trilled, every living thing seemed to be full of sweetness and light. They found a little hat, made of furry brown plush; but it was all moth-eaten. Félicité asked if she might have it. Their eyes met, filled with tears; finally the mistress opened her arms, the servant fell into them; and they embraced, appeasing their grief in a kiss which made them equal.

It was the first time in their lives, for Madame Aubain was not naturally forthcoming. Félicité was as grateful to her as if she had received a gift, and from then on loved her with dog-like devotion and religious adoration.

Her natural kindness began to develop.

When she heard the drums of a regiment marching down the street, she would stand at the door with a jug of cider, offering the soldiers a drink. She looked after cholera victims. She took the Poles* under her wing; and one of them even announced that he would like to marry her. But they fell out; for one morning, coming back from the Angelus service, she found him in her kitchen; he had found his own way in, and dressed himself a salad which he was calmly eating.

After the Poles, it was Père Colmiche, an old man reputed to have committed atrocities in 1793.* He lived by the river in a tumbledown old pigsty. The village boys used to watch him through cracks in the wall, and throw stones which fell on the pallet where he lay, constantly racked by bronchial coughing; he had very long hair, inflamed eyelids and a tumour on the arm bigger than his head. She got him clean linen, tried to clean up his hovel, dreamed about moving him into the bakehouse, without giving Madame Aubain any trouble. When the cancer burst, she dressed it every day, sometimes brought him cake, put him out in the sunshine on a bale of hay; and the poor old fellow, dribbling and shaking, would thank her in his feeble voice, was afraid of losing her, and stretched out his hands as soon as he saw her going. He died; she had a Mass said for the repose of his soul.

On that particular day she had a great stroke of fortune; at dinner-time, Madame de Larsonnière's negro arrived, holding the parrot in its cage, with its perch, chain, and padlock. A note from the Baroness informed Madame Aubain that her husband had been promoted to a Prefecture and they were leaving that evening; and she begged her to accept the bird as a memento and token of her respects.

The parrot had filled Félicité's thoughts for some time past, for it came from America; that word reminded her of Victor, and prompted her to question the negro about it. She had even once said: 'Madame would be so happy to have it!'

The negro had repeated the remark to his mistress, who, being unable to take the bird with her, disposed of it in that way.

III

HE was called Loulou. His body was green, his wingtips pink, the front of his head blue, his breast gold.

But he had the tiresome habit of chewing his perch, pulling out his feathers, scattering his droppings, upsetting the water in his birdbath; Madame Aubain found him a nuisance, and gave him to Félicité for good.

She began training him; soon he could repeat: 'Nice boy! Your servant, Sir! Hail Mary!' He was placed beside the door, and a number of people were surprised that he did not answer to the name of Jacquot,* since all parrots are called Jacquot. They described him as 'silly as a goose, thick as a plank'; Félicité was deeply wounded every time by such remarks. How odd that Loulou should perversely fall speechless as soon as anyone looked at him!

All the same he was eager for company; for on Sundays, while *those* Mesdemoiselles Rochefeuille, Monsieur de Houppeville and some new friends: Onfroy, the apothecary, Monsieur Varin and Captain Mathieu, were playing their game of cards, he would bang the window-panes with his wings and make such a dreadful fuss that one could not hear oneself speak.

There was no doubt that he found Bourais's face very funny. As soon as he saw him Loulou began to laugh and laugh with might and main. His peals of laughter rebounded round the courtyard, the echo repeated them, the neighbours looked out of their windows, laughing too; and to avoid being seen by the parrot, Monsieur Bourais would slink along the wall, hat pulled down to hide his face, go down to the river and then come in by the garden gate; and the looks he gave the bird were anything but affectionate.

The butcher's boy had once given Loulou a smack for taking the liberty of sticking his head into his basket; and ever since Loulou was always trying to nip him through his shirt. Fabu threatened to wring his neck, although he was not really cruel, despite his tattooed arms and heavy whiskers. On the contrary! he had rather a liking for the parrot, and in jovial mood went so far as to teach him some swear-words. Félicité, horrified at such behaviour, put him in the kitchen. His chain was removed, and he had the run of the house.

When he went down the stairs, he would press the curve of his beak against the steps, and raise first his right foot, then the left; and she was afraid that such gymnastics would make him dizzy. He fell ill, could not talk or eat any more. This was due to a callus under his tongue, such as chickens sometimes have. She cured him by peeling off this bit of skin with her nails. One day Monsieur Paul was foolish enough to blow cigar smoke up his nose; another time when Madame

Loumeau was teasing him with the tip of her sunshade he
snapped up the ferrule; finally he got lost.

She had put him down on the grass to take the air, gone
off for a moment, and when she came back, there was no
parrot! First she hunted for him in the bushes, down by the
river, and on the rooftops, paying no heed to her mistress
who was shouting at her: 'Do take care! you must be crazy!'
Then she searched all the gardens of Pont-l'Évêque, and kept
stopping passers-by—'You haven't by any chance seen my
parrot, have you?' If they did not know the parrot, she
described him. Suddenly she thought she could make out
something green, fluttering behind the windmills at the
bottom of the hill. But on top of the hill, there was
nothing! A pedlar told her that he had come across him
a short while ago at Saint-Melaine, in Mère Simon's shop.
She hurried there. They did not know what she was talking
about. At last she came home, exhausted, her slippers torn to
shreds, with death in her heart; she sat down in the middle
of the seat by Madame, and was recounting all her efforts,
when she felt a light touch on her shoulder: Loulou! What
on earth had he been doing? Perhaps he had been on a tour
of the neighbourhood!

She had difficulty getting over this experience, or rather
she never got over it.

Following a chill, she had an attack of quinsy; shortly
afterwards, ear trouble. Three years later she had gone deaf,
and used to talk very loudly, even in church. Although her
sins could have been published in every corner of the diocese
without bringing her into disrepute or upsetting anyone,
Monsieur le curé judged it more suitable in future to hear
her confessions in the sacristy.*

On top of all her other troubles, buzzings in her ears
made her imagine things. Her mistress would often tell her:
'Goodness! how stupid you are!' and she would reply: 'Yes,
Madame', as she looked round for something.

The narrow range of her ideas shrank even further, and the pealing of the bells, the lowing of the cattle ceased to exist for her. Every living thing moved in ghostly silence. A single sound now reached her ears: the voice of the parrot.

As if to entertain her he would reproduce the regular clicking of the spit turning, the fishmonger's shrill cry, the sawing of the carpenter who lived opposite; and when the doorbell rang, he would imitate Madame Aubain: 'Félicité! the door! the door!'

They would hold conversations, he repeating *ad nauseam* the three phrases of his repertory, and she answering with words which were equally disconnected but came from the heart. In her isolation Loulou was almost like a son, a lover to her. He would climb up her fingers, nibble her lips, cling to her bodice; and as she bent forward, wagging her head as nurses do, the wide wings of her bonnet and those of the bird quivered in unison.

When the clouds banked up and thunder rumbled, he would squawk, perhaps remembering the downpours of his native forests. The water streaming down sent him into a frenzy; he would frantically flutter about, go up to the ceiling, knock everything over, and fly out of the window to splash about in the garden; but he would soon come in again, and hopping up and down on one of the firedogs to dry his feathers, displayed his beak and his tail alternately.

One morning in the terrible winter of 1837, she had put him down in front of the hearth because of the cold, when she found him dead, hanging head down in the middle of the cage, his claws clutching the bars. He had probably died of a stroke. She thought he might have been poisoned with parsley;* and despite the lack of any evidence, her suspicions settled on Fabu.

She cried so much that her mistress said to her: 'All right! Have him stuffed!'

She went to ask the pharmacist for advice, as he had always treated the parrot kindly.

He wrote to Le Havre. A certain Fellacher took on the job. But as parcels sent by the mail-coach were sometimes lost, she decided to take this one herself as far as Honfleur.

Leafless apple trees lined either side of the road. The ditches were frozen over. Dogs barked round the farms; and with her hands tucked under her cape, her little black sabots and her bag she walked briskly along the middle of the roadway.

She crossed the forest, passed by Le Haut-Chêne, reached Saint-Gatien.*

Behind her, in a cloud of dust, gathering speed downhill, a mail-coach driven at full gallop hurtled on like a whirlwind. At the sight of this woman who did not move out of the way, the driver stood up above the hood, and the postillion shouted too, while the four horses, which he could not rein in, galloped all the faster; the two leading ones just missed her; with a jerk on the reins he drove them on to the verge, but raising his arm in fury, he lashed out with his great whip, catching her such a mighty blow from waist to head that she fell over backwards.

Her first action on recovering her senses was to open the basket. Fortunately Loulou was unharmed. She felt her right cheek burning; when she touched it her hands came away red. It was bleeding.

She sat down on a pile of stones, dabbed her face with her kerchief, then ate a crust of bread, which she had put in her basket as a precaution, and consoled herself for her injury by looking at the bird.

When she came to the top of the hill at Ecquemauville she could see the lights of Honfleur twinkling in the darkness like a mass of stars; blurred in the distance, the sea stretched out in all directions. Then a sudden weakness made her stop; and her wretched childhood, her first unhappy love affair, her nephew's departure, Virginie's death, all came back to her at once like a rising tide, and welling up in her throat made her choke.

Then she asked to speak to the captain of the boat;* and without telling him what her parcel contained, asked him to take great care of it.

Fellacher kept the parrot for a long time. He was always promising it for the following week; after six months he reported that a box had gone off; that was the last she heard. Loulou would probably never come back. 'They must have stolen him!' she thought.

At last he arrived—looking splendid, standing on a tree branch, which was screwed on to a mahogany pedestal, one foot in the air, head cocked sideways, and biting a nut, which the taxidermist, whose tastes ran to the grandiose, had gilded.

She shut him up in her room.

This place, to which few people were ever admitted, looked like a chapel and a bazaar combined, with its collection of religious objects and assorted oddments.

A large wardrobe obstructed the opening of the door. Facing the window overlooking the garden, another small round one gave on to the courtyard; a table, beside the humble bed, bore a water jug, two combs and a block of blue soap in a chipped dish. On the walls were displayed: rosaries, medals, several pictures of the Virgin, a holy-water stoup fashioned out of a coconut shell; on the chest of drawers, draped like an altar with a cloth, the seashell box that Victor had given her; then a watering-can and a ball, some exercise-books, the geography picture-book, a pair of bootees; and hanging from the nail that held the mirror the little plush hat! Félicité carried this sort of respect so far that she even kept one of Monsieur's frock-coats. All the old odds and ends for which Madame Aubain had no further use were picked up by Félicité for her room. That is how there came to be artificial flowers along the edge of the chest of drawers, and a portrait of the Comte d'Artois* in the window recess.

Loulou was installed on a small shelf fixed on to a chimney-breast which projected into the room. Every morning as she awoke she saw him by the first light of day, and would then recall the days gone by and the smallest details of unimportant events, without sorrow, quite serenely.

Never communicating with anyone, she lived with senses dulled as if sleepwalking. The Corpus Christi processions would bring her back to life. She would call on the neighbours to collect candlesticks and mats to embellish the altar of repose being set up in the street.

In church she always gazed at the Holy Spirit, and noticed that he looked something like the parrot. The likeness seemed still more evident in a popular print of Our Lord's baptism. With his purple wings and emerald green body he was the very image of Loulou.

She bought the print and hung it up in place of the Comte d'Artois, with the result that she could take them in together with a single glance. They became associated in her mind, so that the parrot became sanctified from this connexion with the Holy Spirit, which in turn became more lifelike and readily intelligible in her eyes. The Father could never have chosen to express himself through a dove, for those creatures cannot speak, but rather one of Loulou's ancestors. And Félicité would look at the print as she said her prayers, but with a sidelong glance from time to time at the bird.

She wanted to join the Children of Mary.* Madame Aubain talked her out of it.

An important event was suddenly in the offing: Paul's marriage.

He had been first a lawyer's clerk, then in trade, in the Customs, in the Revenue, and had begun an application to

the Waterways and Forests Department; now, at thirty, by
some heaven-sent inspiration, he had suddenly discovered
the right path: Registration Office* for Deeds! There he
demonstrated such remarkable talents that an auditor had
offered him his daughter's hand, and promised to take him
under his wing.

Paul, who now took life seriously, brought her to visit his
mother.

She sneered at the way things were done at Pont-l'Évêque,
acted high and mighty, upset Félicité. Madame Aubain felt a
sense of relief when she left.

The following week came news of Monsieur Bourais's
death, in Lower Brittany, in an inn. Rumours of suicide
were confirmed; doubts were raised as to his honesty.
Madame Aubain examined her accounts, and it was not long
before she became aware of the catalogue of his infamies:
embezzlement of arrears, disguised sales of timber, forged
receipts, etc. In addition he had fathered a natural child, and
had had 'relations with a person from Dozulé'.*

Such base conduct grieved her deeply. In March 1853 she
suddenly felt pains in her chest; her tongue seemed to have an
opaque coating, leeches did nothing to relieve the difficulty
in breathing; and on the ninth evening she expired, being just
seventy-two years old.

People thought she was younger, because of her brown
hair, worn in coils round her pale, pockmarked face. Few
friends missed her, for her haughty ways put people off.

Félicité wept for her, but not just as a servant for an
employer. The idea that Madame should die before her
she found disturbing, against the natural order of things,
unacceptable and monstrous.

Ten days later—the time it took to hurry there from
Besançon—the heirs arrived. The daughter-in-law ran-
sacked the drawers, picked out some pieces of furniture, sold
the rest, and then they went back to the Registration Office.

Madame's easy chair, her pedestal table, her footwarmer, the eight upright chairs had all gone. Yellow squares in the middle of the walls marked where the prints had been. They had taken the two children's cots, with their mattresses, and every trace of Virginie's things had vanished from the cupboard! Félicité went back upstairs, sick with grief.

Next day there was a notice on the door; the apothecary shouted in her ear that the house was for sale.

She reeled, and was obliged to sit down.

What grieved her most was the thought of having to leave her room—so convenient for poor Loulou. Gazing at him in anguish, she implored the help of the Holy Spirit, and fell into the idolatrous habit of saying her prayers on her knees in front of the parrot. Sometimes the sun coming through the skylight would catch his glass eye, so that a great beam of light flashed out from it, and this entranced her.

She had been left an annuity of 380 francs by her mistress. The garden provided her with vegetables. As for clothes, she had enough to wear for the rest of her days, and saved the cost of lighting by going to bed as soon as it was dusk.

She hardly ever went out, to avoid the secondhand shop, where some of the furniture from the house was on display. Since her dizzy spells, she was lame in one leg; and as she grew weaker, Mère Simon, whose grocery shop had come to grief, came in every morning to chop wood and pump water for her.

Her sight began to go. The shutters were never open any more. Many years went by. The house remained unlet and unsold.

For fear of being evicted Félicité never asked for repairs. The roof laths became rotten; for the whole of one winter her bolster was soaked. After Easter she began spitting blood.

At that Mère Simon called in the doctor. Félicité wanted to know what was wrong with her. But she was too deaf to hear the answer, and caught just one word: 'Pneumonia.'

That was a word she knew, and she softly replied: 'Oh! like Madame', finding it perfectly natural to follow her mistress.

The time for the altars of repose was drawing near.

The first was always at the bottom of the hill, the second in front of the post office, the third about halfway up the street. There were rival claims for that one; the ladies of the parish finally chose Madame Aubain's courtyard.

The fever got worse, and she found it harder and harder to breathe. Félicité was distressed that she was not doing anything for the altar. At the very least she could have put something on it! Then she thought of the parrot. It was not suitable; the neighbours objected. But the curé granted permission; that made her so happy that she begged him to accept Loulou, the only valuable thing she owned, when she died.

From the Tuesday to the Saturday, the eve of Corpus Christi, she coughed more frequently. By evening her face was drawn with illness, her lips stuck to her gums, she began to vomit; and first thing next morning she had a priest called.

Three women stood round her during the administration of Extreme Unction. Then she announced that she needed to speak to Fabu.

He arrived in his Sunday best, ill at ease in this funereal atmosphere.

'Forgive me,' she said, making an effort to stretch out her arm, 'I thought it was you who killed him!'

What could such nonsense mean? Suspecting him of murder, a man like him! And he waxed indignant, was about to make a fuss. 'Her mind's begun to wander, anyone can see that!'

Félicité spoke from time to time to shadows. The good women left. Old Mère Simon had her lunch.

A little later she took Loulou, and bringing him close to Félicité said:

'Now then! Say goodbye to him!'

Although he was not a corpse, he was all worm-eaten, one of his wings was broken, the stuffing was coming out of his stomach. But now quite blind, she kissed his head and held him against her cheek. Mère Simon took him back, to put him on the altar of repose.

V

FROM the meadows rose the scent of summer; flies buzzed; the sun glinted on the river, warmed the slates. Mère Simon had come back into the room and was quietly dozing.

The sound of bells ringing woke her up; they were coming out of Vespers. Félicité's delirium calmed down. As she thought about the procession, she could see it as if she had been following it.

All the schoolchildren, the choristers, and the fire brigade walked on the pavements, while down the middle of the street advanced first the uniformed verger, armed with his halberd, then the beadle with a great cross, the schoolmaster superintending the boys, the nun fussing over her little girls; three of the prettiest, with curly hair like angels, were throwing rose petals up in the air; the deacon, with arms outstretched, conducted the band; and two thurifers turned round at every step towards the Blessed Sacrament, borne by Monsieur le curé in his splendid chasuble, beneath a canopy of crimson velvet carried by four churchwardens. A throng of people pressed on behind, between the white cloths hung out over the walls of the houses; and they came to the foot of the hill.

A cold sweat bathed Félicité's temples. Mère Simon wiped it off with a cloth, telling herself that one day she would have to go through it too.

The noise from the crowd swelled, was very loud for a moment, faded away.

A volley of shots rattled the windows. It was the postillions* saluting the monstrance. Félicité rolled her eyes, and said, as loudly as she could, 'Is he all right?'—worrying about the parrot.

Her death agony began. Laboured breathing, coming faster and faster, made her sides heave. Bubbles of froth formed at the corners of her mouth, and she was trembling all over.

Soon the booming of the ophicleides could be heard, the clear voices of the children, the deeper tones of the men. They all fell silent now and then, and the tramping of feet, deadened by flowers strewn on the ground, sounded like a herd of cattle moving over grass.

The clergy appeared in the courtyard. Mère Simon climbed on a chair to reach the little round window, so that she could look down on to the altar of repose.

Garlands of greenery hung on the altar, which was decorated with a frill of English lace. In the middle was a small frame containing relics, two orange trees stood at the corners, and all the way along were silver candlesticks and china vases, from which projected sunflowers, lilies, peonies, foxgloves, bunches of hydrangea. This pile of bright colours sloped down diagonally from the first floor to the carpet spread over the paving stones; and some rare objects caught the eye. A silver-gilt sugar bowl had a wreath of violets, pendants of Alençon gemstones sparkled on a bed of moss, two Chinese screens displayed landscapes. All that could be seen of Loulou, hidden beneath some roses, was the blue front of his head, like a plaque of lapis-lazuli.

The churchwardens, the choristers, the children, formed up round the three sides of the courtyard. The priest slowly mounted the steps and set on the lace the great golden sun, which shone radiantly. All knelt. There was a great silence. Then the censers, swung with might and main, slid up and down their chains.

A cloud of blue incense smoke rose up to Félicité's room. She opened wide her nostrils as she breathed it in deeply, in an act at once sensual and mystical. She closed her eyes. Her lips smiled. Her heartbeats grew steadily slower, fainter every time, softer, like a fountain running dry, like an echo fading; and as she breathed her last, she thought she saw, as the heavens opened, a gigantic parrot hovering over her head.

The Legend of Saint Julian
the Hospitaller

JULIAN's father and mother lived in a castle, in the middle of the forest, on the slope of a hill.

The towers at each of the four corners had pointed roofs covered with lead in a pattern of scales, and the base of the walls rested on slabs of rock, which plunged down steeply to the bottom of the moat.

The paving of the courtyard was as clean as the floor of a church. Long waterspouts, in the shape of dragons with their jaws pointing downwards, spat out rainwater into the storage tank, and on the windowsills, on every floor, in a pot of painted clay, bloomed a basil or a heliotrope.

A second enclosure, composed of stakes, contained first a fruit orchard, then a flower bed, with combinations of flowers forming patterns, then a trellised walk, with arbours where one could take the air, and a pall-mall alley for the recreation of the pages. On the other side lay the kennels, stables, bakery, wine-press and granaries. A green pasture spread out all round, enclosed in its turn by a stout thorn-hedge.

They had lived in peace for so long that the portcullis was not lowered any more; the moat was overgrown with grass; swallows nested in the slits of the battlements; and the archer who patrolled the castle walls all day long withdrew to the watchtower as soon as the sun's heat became too much for him, and there dropped off to sleep like a monk in his stall.

Everywhere inside ironwork gleamed; tapestries hung in the rooms as a protection against the cold; the cupboards were stacked with linen, great barrels of wine were piled up in the cellars, oak chests creaked under the weight of money-bags.

In the armoury, between the standards and the wild-animal heads, could be seen weapons of every age and nation, from Amalekite* slings and Garamant javelins to Saracen broadswords and Norman coats of mail.

On the main spit in the kitchen one could roast an ox; the chapel was as sumptuous as the oratory of a king. There was even, in a secluded place, a Roman steam bath; but the good lord did without it, considering such a practice fit only for idolaters.

Always wrapped in a fox-fur mantle, he would walk round his home, dispensing justice to his vassals and acting as peacemaker in his neighbours' quarrels. In winter-time he would watch the snowflakes fall, or have someone read him stories. With the coming of the first fine weather he would ride off on his mule along the byways, beside the fields where the corn sprouted green, chatting to the peasants and giving them advice. After many adventures he had taken to wife a lady of high degree.

She was very fair-skinned, somewhat aloof and serious. The points of her tall hennin* brushed against the lintel of the doorways, the train of her fine woollen gown swept three paces behind her. Her household routine was as regular as that of a monastery; every morning she assigned tasks to her serving-women, supervised the making of preserves and ointments, span on her distaff or embroidered altar cloths. At length her prayers were answered and she bore a son.

At that there was much rejoicing, and a banquet lasting three days and four nights, lit by torches, to the sound of harps, with leafy branches strewn on the floor. They ate the rarest spices, with chickens as big as sheep; for their entertainment a dwarf emerged from a pie; and when there were no longer enough bowls for the ever-growing throng, they were obliged to drink from ivory horns and helmets.

The newly delivered mother did not attend these festivities, She stayed quietly in bed. One evening she woke up, and in a moonbeam shining in through the window she saw something like a shadow moving. It was an old man in a rough habit, beads at his side, pouch on his shoulder, looking just like a hermit. He came up to her bedside and said, without opening his lips:

'Mother, rejoice! Your son will be a saint!'

She was about to cry out, but slipping along the moonbeam he gently rose into the air, then disappeared. The singing from the banquet broke out louder than ever. She heard angel voices; her head fell back on the pillow, above which hung a martyr's bone framed in carbuncle stones.

Next day all the servants were questioned; they swore that they had not seen any hermit. Dream or reality, it must have been a message from heaven; but she was careful to say nothing about it, for fear of being accused of pride.

The guests went off at daybreak, and Julian's father was outside the postern gate, where he had just seen off the last of them, when suddenly a beggar stood before him in the haze. He was a gipsy, with braided beard, silver bracelets on his arms, and flashing eyes. He stammered out like a man inspired these disjointed words:

'Ah, ah, your son . . .! much blood! . . . much glory . . .! Always good fortune! An emperor's family!'

And, bending down to pick up his alms, he disappeared in the grass and vanished.

The good castellan looked to right and left, called out at the top of his voice. No one! The wind whistled, the morning mists dispersed.

He put this vision down to a head weary from lack of sleep. 'If I talk about it, people will laugh at me,' he said to himself. However, the brilliant future predicted for his son dazzled him, although the promise was far from clear, and he even doubted whether he had really heard it.

Husband and wife hid their secret from each other, but both loved and cherished the child equally, and respecting him as someone marked out by God, they treated him with the utmost consideration. His little bed was stuffed with the finest down; a lamp shaped like a dove constantly burned above it; three nurses rocked him, and wrapped up in his swaddling clothes, with his rosy cheeks and blue eyes, his brocade coat and his bonnet sewn with pearls, he looked like an infant Jesus. He cut his teeth without crying once.

When he was seven his mother taught him to sing. To make him brave, his father hoisted him on to a big horse. The child smiled with delight, and it was not long before he knew all about chargers.

A very learned old monk taught him Holy Scripture, the Arabic system of numbers,* Latin literature, and the art of painting miniatures on vellum. They worked together, at the very top of a turret, away from any noise.

When lessons were over, they would go down into the garden, where they paced about, studying the flowers.

Sometimes one could see wending their way down through the valley a line of pack-animals, led by a man on foot dressed in Eastern fashion. The castellan, recognizing him as a merchant, would send a servant after him. Reassured, the stranger would turn off his route; and shown into the parlour, he would take out of his chests bolts of velvet and silk, examples of the goldsmith's art, herbs and spices, and singular things for unknown use; in the end the good man would leave with a fat profit, and unharmed. At other times a band of pilgrims would knock at the door. Their wet clothes would steam in front of the hearth, and when they had been fed, they would describe their journeys: sailing over foam-flecked seas, walking across burning sands, the savagery of the paynim, the Syrian caves, the Manger and

the Holy Sepulchre. Then they would give the young lord
the pilgrim shells* from their cloaks.

The castellan would often entertain his old comrades in
arms. As they drank, they would recall their wars, assaults
on fortresses, with the battering of the siege engines and
fearful wounds. Julian would cry out as he listened to them;
then his father had no doubt that later on he would be a
conqueror. But in the evening, as he came out from the
Angelus service* and passed between the poor with heads
bent low, he would dip into his purse with such modesty
and such nobility that his mother fully expected to see him
one day an archbishop.

His place in the chapel was beside his parents, and
however long the service might last, he would stay kneeling
at his prie-Dieu, with his cap on the ground and his hands
joined in prayer.

One day, during Mass, he noticed as he raised his head
a little white mouse coming out of a hole in the wall. It
scampered on to the first altar step, and after turning two or
three times to right and left, ran back in the same direction.
The following Sunday he was disturbed at the idea that he
might see it again. It did come back; and every Sunday he
would wait for it and find it irritating, until he began to hate
it and resolved to get rid of it.

So, shutting the door, he sprinkled cake crumbs over the
steps, and posted himself in front of the hole, with a stick
in his hand.

After a very long while a pink nose appeared, followed
by the whole mouse. He struck it a light blow, and stood
astounded in front of the little body, which no longer
moved. A drop of blood stained the flagstones. He quickly
wiped it off with his sleeve, threw the mouse outside and
said nothing about it to anyone.

All kinds of little birds used to peck up seeds in the
garden. He had the idea of putting peas into a hollow reed.

When he heard twittering in a tree, he would come up softly, then raise his tube and puff out his cheeks, and the little creatures would rain down on his shoulders so thick and fast that he could not help laughing with pleasure at his mischief.

One morning, as he was coming back along the castle wall, he saw on the ridge of the rampart a plump pigeon puffing out its chest in the sun. Julian stopped to watch it; as there was a breach in the wall at that point, he found a bit of stone beneath his fingers. He swung his arm, and the stone knocked down the bird, which plummeted down into the moat.

He rushed headlong down to the bottom, tearing himself on the brushwood, nosing everywhere, more nimbly than a young hound.

The pigeon, with broken wings, hung trembling in the branches of a privet.

Its persistent hold on life angered the boy. He began to throttle it, and the bird's convulsions made his heart beat faster, filling him with wild, turbulent ecstasy. When it finally grew stiff he felt quite faint.

That evening during supper his father declared that his son was now of an age when he ought to learn the art of venery, and he went to find an old copybook containing in question and answer form a complete guide to the chase.* In it a master set out for his pupil the art of training hounds and breaking in falcons, setting traps, recognizing a stag from its fumets, the fox from its prints, the wolf from its scratchings on the ground, the right way to distinguish their spoors, how to flush them from cover, where to find their usual lairs, the most favourable winds, with a list of the cries and rules for dividing the spoils.

When Julian could recite all these things off by heart, his father put together for him a pack of hounds.

First there were twenty-four Barbary greyhounds, swifter than gazelles, but liable to bolt out of control; then seventeen pairs of Breton dogs, mottled white on red, unfailingly obedient, great barkers with powerful chests. For attacking wild boar and dangerous coverts, there were forty griffons, as shaggy as bears. Fiery-red Tartar mastiffs, almost as tall as asses, with broad backs and straight hocks, were intended for pursuing bison. The spaniels' black coats shone like satin; the talbots yelped as loudly as the tuneful beagles. In a separate yard eight alan hounds growled, rattling their chains and rolling their eyes; formidable beasts which can leap as high as a horseman's belly and are not afraid of lions.

They ate good wheaten bread, drank from stone troughs and each bore some resounding name.

The collection of falcons perhaps surpassed the pack of hounds; the good lord spent freely to acquire Caucasian tiercelets, Babylonian sakers, German gerfalcons, and peregrines caught on cliffs beside icy seas in far-off lands. They were kept in a thatched shed, fastened to the perch in order of size, and in front of them was a bank of turf on which they were put from time to time to stretch their wings.

Purse-nets, caltrops, hooks, all kinds of contraptions were constructed.

They often went out into the country after wildfowl, and the dogs were quick to point. Then the beaters came steadily forward, carefully spreading out a huge net over the dogs' motionless bodies. At a word of command, they began to bark, the quail flew up, and the ladies from round about who had been invited with their husbands, the children, the ladies' maids, everyone, leaped on them and caught them with the greatest ease. At other times they would beat a drum to flush out hares; foxes would fall into pits, or a wolf, setting off a spring-trap, would be caught by the foot.

But Julian scorned such handy devices; he preferred to hunt far from other people, with his horse and his hawk.

It was almost always a great snow-white Tartary falcon from Scythia. Its leather hood had a plume on top, little golden bells tinkled on its blue feet, and it held firmly on to its master's arm as the horse galloped over the unfolding plains. Julian would loose its jesses, and suddenly let it go; the creature rose boldly up into the air, straight as an arrow, and one would see two spots of unequal size turn, merge, then disappear high up in the blue sky. It would not be long before the falcon came down, tearing some other bird to pieces, and landed back on his gauntlet with quivering wings.

In like manner Julian flew the heron, the kite, the crow and the vulture.

He liked to sound his horn as he followed his dogs, running up hillsides, jumping over brooks, going back into the forest; and when the stag began to moan from the pain of their bites, he would swiftly despatch it, and then delight in the frenzy of the hounds as they devoured their prey, cut into pieces, on the steaming hide.

On misty days he would drive deep into a marsh to watch for geese, otter, and wild duck.

Three squires would be waiting for him from daybreak at the foot of the terrace, and the old monk, leaning out of his window, would beckon him home in vain: Julian did not return. He would go out in the heat of the sun, in rain or in storm, drinking spring-water from his cupped hand, eating wild apples as he trotted along; if he was tired, he would rest beneath an oak tree, and come back in the middle of the night, covered in mud and blood, his hair full of thorns, and reeking of wild animals. He became like them. When his mother greeted him with a kiss, he responded coldly to her embrace and seemed to be absorbed in matters of great moment.

He killed bears with a knife, bulls with an axe, wild boar with a spear, and once, having only a stick left, even defended himself against some wolves gnawing at corpses at the foot of a gibbet.

One winter morning he set out before dawn, well equipped, with a crossbow over his shoulder and a supply of arrows at his saddlebow. His Danish jennet, followed by two basset hounds, made the ground ring beneath its steady stride. Drops of ice stuck to his cloak, it was blowing a gale. On one side the horizon grew lighter, and in the pale half-light he noticed some rabbits hopping around near their burrows. The two bassets at once rushed at them and swiftly snapped a spine or two.

Soon he entered a wood. A wood-grouse, stiff with cold, was sleeping at the end of a branch, its head tucked under its wing. With a backward slash of his sword Julian severed its two feet and went on his way without picking it up.

Three hours later he found himself on a mountain peak so high that the sky looked almost black. In front of him a rock like a long wall plunged down, overhanging a precipice; and at the far end two wild goats looked into the abyss. As he did not have his arrows with him, for his horse had stayed behind, he decided to go down to them; crouching and barefoot he finally reached the first goat and plunged a dagger under its ribs. The second leaped terrified into the void. Julian dashed forward to strike it, his right foot slipped, and he fell on to the other's carcass, with his face over the abyss and arms spread out.

Going down into the plain again, he followed some willows lining a river. Cranes, flying very low, passed over his head from time to time. Julian knocked them down with his whip and did not miss one.

Meanwhile the warmer air had melted the frost, large patches of mist floated in the air, and the sun came out. Far off he saw a lake, its surface so smooth that it had the sheen of lead. In the middle of the lake was an animal that Julian did not recognize, a beaver with a black muzzle. Despite the distance, an arrow killed it, and Julian was only sorry that he could not take the pelt.

Then he advanced through an avenue of great trees, whose lofty tops formed a kind of triumphal arch at the entrance to a forest. A roebuck bounded out of a thicket, a fallow deer appeared at an intersection, a badger came out of its sett, a peacock on the grass spread out its tail; and when he had killed them all, more roebuck appeared, more fallow deer, more badgers, more peacocks, and blackbirds, jays, polecats, foxes, hedgehogs, lynx, creatures in endless profusion, more numerous with every step. They turned around him trembling, their eyes full of gentle entreaty. But Julian never wearied of slaughter, successively drawing his crossbow, unsheathing his sword, stabbing with his cutlass, heedless and oblivious of everything. He was out hunting, he knew not where, nor for how long, all he knew was the fact of his own existence, and everything was happening as easily as in a dream. An extraordinary sight brought him up short. Some stags filled a valley shaped like an amphitheatre; and, huddling close together, they warmed each other with their breath, which rose steaming in the haze.

For a few minutes the prospect of such carnage made him choke with pleasure. Then he dismounted from his horse, rolled up his sleeves and began shooting.

As the first arrow whistled by, all the stags turned their heads with one accord. Gaps appeared in their ranks; plaintive cries rose up and the herd shook with a great shudder.

The rim of the valley was too high to pass over. They sprang about in the enclosed space, trying to escape. Julian aimed, fired; and the arrows slashed down like rain in a thunderstorm. The stags fought together in their frenzy, reared up, mounted each other; their bodies, with their antlers tangled together, formed a great pile, which kept collapsing as it moved.

At last they died, lying on the sand, frothing at the mouth, their entrails hanging out, their heaving bellies gradually subsiding. Then all was still.

Darkness was about to fall; and behind the wood, in the gaps between the branches, the sky was as red as a pool of blood.

Julian leaned against a tree. He gazed wide-eyed at the enormity of the massacre, without understanding how he could have done it.

On the other side of the valley, on the edge of the forest, he saw a stag, a doe, and her fawn.

The stag, which was black and of monstrous size, carried sixteen antlers, and had a white tuft of beard. The doe, as light in colour as dead leaves, was grazing the turf; and the dappled fawn clung to her teat without interrupting her progress.

The bow twanged once more. The fawn was killed at once. Then its mother, head raised towards the heavens, let out a harsh cry, deep, heart-rending, human. Angered, Julian brought her down with a shot full in the chest.

The great stag had seen him and sprang forward. Julian shot his last arrow at him. It struck him in the forehead, and stayed embedded there.

The great stag did not seem to feel it; stepping over the dead bodies, he kept coming on, was going to charge him, rip him open; and Julian retreated in unspeakable horror. The monstrous beast stopped; then with blazing eyes, solemn as a patriarch or a judge, to the sound of a bell ringing in the distance, he repeated three times:

'Cursed! cursed! cursed! One day, savage heart, you will murder your father and your mother!'

He bent his knees, slowly closed his eyes, and died.

Julian was stunned, then overwhelmed by sudden weariness; revulsion, immense sorrow swept over him. With his head in his hands he wept for a long time.

His horse was lost, his dogs had abandoned him; the solitude surrounding him seemed full of menace and nameless dangers. Then, driven by dread, he fled through the countryside, chose a path at random, and almost immediately found himself at the castle gate.

That night he did not sleep. By the flickering light of the hanging lamp, he kept seeing the great black stag. The prediction obsessed him; he struggled against it. 'No! no! no! I could never kill them!' Then he thought: 'But supposing I wanted to? . . .' and was afraid that the Devil might prompt such a wish.

For three months his anguished mother prayed beside his bed, and his father constantly walked groaning through the corridors. He sent for the most famous master physicians, who prescribed all kinds of drugs. Julian's sickness, they said, was caused by some deadly wind, or an amorous passion. But to every question the young man replied with a shake of the head.

His strength came back; and he was taken out to walk in the courtyard, with the old monk and the good lord supporting his arms on either side.

When he had completely recovered, he firmly refused to go out hunting.

His father, wanting to give him pleasure, presented him with a great Saracen sword.

It was at the top of a pillar, in a display of weapons. A ladder was needed to reach it. Julian climbed up. The sword was too heavy and slipped from his fingers, and as it fell grazed the good lord so closely that it ripped his cloak. Julian thought he had killed his father, and fainted.

Thenceforth he had a fear of weapons. The sight of a naked blade made him go pale. Such a weakness deeply grieved his family.

Finally the old monk, in the name of God, honour, and his forebears, bade him resume the activities of a nobleman.

Every day the squires amused themselves with throwing the javelin. Julian soon excelled at it. He could aim his into the necks of bottles, break the teeth of weather-vanes, hit studs in the gates at a hundred paces.

One summer evening, at the hour when mist makes things indistinct, he was beneath the trellis in the garden when he saw right at the end two white wings fluttering level with the espalier. He never doubted that it was a stork, and threw his javelin.

A piercing cry rang out.

It was his mother, whose tall hennin, with its long side panels, stayed pinned to the wall.

Julian fled from the castle, never to return.

II

HE enlisted in a troop of soldiers of fortune who were passing by.

He knew hunger, thirst, fevers, and vermin. The wind tanned his skin. His limbs grew tougher from contact with armour; and as he was very strong, brave, moderate, and sensible he easily won command of a company.

At the start of a battle he would urge his soldiers on with a great flourish of his sword. He would use a knotted rope to scale the walls of citadels at night, swaying in the gale, while sparks from the Greek fire stuck to his breastplate, and boiling pitch and molten lead streamed down from the ramparts. Often a stone would smash his shield. Bridges too heavily laden with men collapsed beneath him. Whirling his mace about him he once disposed of fourteen horsemen. In the lists he defeated every challenger who came forward. A score of times or more he was reckoned dead.

Thanks to divine favour he always escaped; for he protected churchmen, orphans, widows, and especially old men. When he saw one walking in front of him, he would call out to see what he looked like, as if afraid of killing him by mistake.

Runaway slaves, rebellious peasants, penniless bastards, dauntless fellows of every kind, flocked to his banner, and he built up an army.

It grew. He became famous. He was much in demand.

He aided successively the Dauphin of France and the King of England, the Templars of Jerusalem, the Surena* of the Parthians, the Negus of Abyssinia and the Emperor of Calicut. He fought Scandinavians covered in fish-scales, negroes equipped with targes of hippopotamus hide riding red asses, golden-skinned Indians brandishing above their diadems great sabres shining brighter than glass. He vanquished Troglodytes and Anthropophagi. He passed through regions so torrid that men's hair flared up in the burning sun like torches; and others so glacial that their arms broke off from their bodies and dropped to the ground; and lands so foggy that they marched with phantoms all around.

States in difficulties consulted him. In his interviews with envoys he obtained unhoped-for terms. If a monarch was behaving too badly, Julian would suddenly arrive and administer a reprimand. He set peoples free. He liberated queens shut up in towers. It was he and no other who slew the wyvern of Milan* and the dragon of Oberbirbach.*

Now the Emperor of Occitania,* after his triumph over the Moors of Spain, had taken as concubine the sister of the Caliph of Cordoba, and by her had had a daughter, whom he had kept and brought up as a Christian. But the Caliph, pretending that he wanted to convert, came to visit him with a numerous escort, massacred his whole garrison, and threw him into a deep dungeon, where he treated him harshly in order to extract from him the location of his treasure.

Julian hastened to his aid, destroyed the pagan army, laid siege to the city, killed the Caliph, cut off his head and tossed it like a bowl over the ramparts. Then he released the Emperor from his prison, and put him back on his throne in the presence of all his court.

To reward him for such a service, the Emperor presented him with baskets full of money; Julian would not accept any. Thinking he wanted more, the Emperor offered him three-quarters of his wealth; a further refusal; then a share of his kingdom; Julian declined with thanks; the Emperor was weeping with vexation, not knowing how to show his gratitude, when he smote his brow, spoke a word in a courtier's ear; the curtains of a wall-hanging were lifted, and a young girl appeared.

Her huge dark eyes shone like two soft lamps. Her lips were parted in a charming smile. The ringlets of her hair caught on the jewels of her half-open gown; and beneath her transparent tunic one could picture her youthful figure. She was quite adorable, well-rounded with a slender waist.

Julian was dazzled with love, all the more so as he had up till then lived very chastely.

So he was given the Emperor's daughter in marriage, with a castle which came to her from her mother; and once the wedding was over, the couple took their leave, after exchanging endless courtesies.

It was a white marble palace, built in Moorish style, on a headland, in an orange grove. Flowery terraces ran down to the shores of a bay, where pink shells crushed underfoot. Behind the castle stretched out a forest in the shape of a fan. The sky was a constant blue, and the trees bent in turn to the sea-breezes and the wind from the mountains which formed the distant horizon.

The shady rooms were brightened by the inlaid walls. Tall pillars, slim as reeds, supported the vaulted cupolas, decorated with reliefs which imitated stalactites in grottoes.

There were fountains playing in the halls, mosaics in the courtyards, festooned partitions, a profusion of architectural refinements, and everywhere such silence that one could hear the rustling of a scarf or the echo of a sigh.

Julian no longer waged war. He took his ease, surrounded by a peaceful people; and every day a throng passed before him, genuflecting and handkissing in the oriental manner.

Clothed in purple, he would stand leaning at a window embrasure, recalling the hunting days of his past; and he would have liked to run after gazelles and ostriches in the desert, hide in the bamboo waiting for leopards, go through forests full of rhinoceros, climb the most inaccessible mountain-peaks the better to aim at eagles, and fight with polar bears on the ice floes in the sea.

Sometimes in a dream he would see himself like our forefather Adam in the midst of Paradise, among all the animals: stretching out his arm, he would put them to death; or else, they would file past, two by two, in order of size, from elephants and lions down to stoats and ducks, as on the day when they went into Noah's ark. From the shadow of a cave he would hurl at them javelins that never missed; others would appear; there was no end to it; and he would wake up with his eyes rolling wildly.

Princely friends invited him over to hunt. He always refused, believing that by this sort of penance he could avert disaster; for it seemed to him that his parents' fate depended on whether or not he killed animals. But it hurt him not to see them, and his other craving became intolerable.

To entertain him, his wife brought in minstrels and dancing girls.

She would go with him in an open litter out into the countryside; at other times, lying in a boat, they would watch the fish roaming in water as clear as the sky. She would often throw flowers in his face; crouching at his feet she would play tunes on a mandoline with three strings; then, laying her clasped hands on his shoulder, she would shyly say:

'What ails you, dear my lord?'

He would either not answer or burst into sobs; one day he finally confessed the horror that lay on his mind.

She countered it with logical arguments: his father and mother were probably dead; if he were ever to see them again, by what chance, to what end, could he possibly commit such an abominable deed? Thus his fears were groundless, and he should take up hunting again.

Julian listened to her with a smile, but could not bring himself to satisfy his desire.

One evening in August when they were in their room, she had just gone to bed and he was kneeling to say his prayers, when he heard a fox bark, then light steps beneath the window; and in the shadows he caught a glimpse of what looked like animals. The temptation was too strong. He took down his quiver.

She looked surprised.

'I am doing your bidding!' he said. 'I shall be back by sunrise.'

Yet she feared some calamity.

He reassured her, then went out, amazed at the inconsistency of her mood.

Shortly afterwards a page came to announce that two strangers, in the absence of the lord, were asking to see his lady straight away.

And soon an old man and an old woman came into the room, backs bent, covered in dust, dressed in coarse linen, each leaning on a stick.

They found the courage to assert that they brought Julian news of his parents.

She bent forward to hear them.

But, exchanging a glance of complicity, they asked if he still loved his parents, if he ever spoke about them.

'Oh yes!' she said.

Then they cried:

'Well! that is who we are!' and they sat down, being very

weary and exhausted.

The young woman had no reason to believe that her husband was their son.

They proved that it was so by describing distinguishing marks on his skin.

She jumped out of bed, summoned her page, and they were served a meal.

Although they were very hungry, they could scarcely eat; and she covertly observed how their bony hands trembled as they picked up their beakers.

They asked innumerable questions about Julian. She answered every one, but was careful to say nothing about his morbid fears concerning them.

When they saw that he was not coming back, they had left their castle; and they had been travelling for many years, on the vaguest indications, without ever losing hope. It had cost so much to pay ferry tolls, and wayside inns, taxes imposed by rulers, and the demands of robbers, that there was no money left in their purse, and now they were reduced to begging. What did that matter since they would soon be embracing their son? They lauded his good fortune in having so gracious a wife, and did not tire of gazing at her and kissing her.

They were much astonished at the luxury of the apartments, and the old man, after examining the walls, asked why they bore the arms of the Emperor of Occitania.

She replied: 'He is my father!'

At that he started, remembering the Gipsy's prophecy; and the old woman thought of the Hermit's words. No doubt her son's present distinction was only the first glimmer of eternal glory, and both remained open-mouthed, by the light of the candelabra which lit up the table.

They must have been very good-looking when they were young. The mother still had all her hair, which hung in fine coils, like patches of snow, down below her cheeks; and the father, with his tall figure and long beard, looked like a statue in a church.

Julian's wife urged them not to wait up for him. She put them to bed herself, in her own bed, then closed the casement; they fell asleep. Day was about to break, and behind the glass, the little birds were beginning to sing.

Julian had crossed the park; and he was walking briskly through the forest, enjoying the softness of the turf and the mildness of the air.

The shadows of the trees stretched out over the moss. Sometimes the moon cast patches of whiteness on to the clearings, and he hesitated to go on, thinking that what he saw was a pool of water, sometimes the surface of still ponds blended into the colour of the grass. Everywhere a great silence reigned; and he could not find any of the animals which only a few minutes earlier had been roaming round his castle.

The forest grew denser, the darkness deeper. Gusts of warm wind blew, full of enervating scents. He kept plunging into piles of dead leaves, and leaned against an oak to get his breath back.

Suddenly behind his back a darker mass sprang up; a wild boar. Julian did not have time to grasp his bow; this upset him as much as a real disaster would have done.

Then, leaving the forest, he saw a wolf hurrying along a hedge.

Julian shot an arrow at it. The wolf stopped, turned to look at him, and continued on its way. It trotted along, always keeping the same distance, stopping from time to time, and as soon as it became a target, running away again.

In this way Julian passed over an endless plain, then some sandhills, and at length found himself on a plateau overlooking a large expanse of country. Flat stones were scattered among ruined vaults. He stumbled over the bones of the dead; here and there worm-eaten crosses leaned over piteously. But shapes moved in the indistinct shadow of the tombs; and some hyenas sprang out, panting with alarm. They came up and sniffed at him, their claws clicking on the flagstones, snarling and showing their teeth. He unsheathed his sword. They all ran off in different directions and rushed on with their limping gallop until they disappeared in a cloud of dust in the distance.

An hour later in a ravine he came across a maddened bull, horns lowered in fury and pawing the sand with its hoofs. Julian drove in his lance under its dewlaps. It splintered, as if the animal were made of bronze; he closed his eyes, awaiting death. When he opened them again, the bull had vanished.

Then his spirit broke with shame. Some higher power was destroying his strength; and, turning back home, he entered the forest again.

It was tangled with creepers; and while he was cutting them with his sword, a stone-marten suddenly slipped between his legs, a panther sprang over his shoulder, a snake coiled up an ash tree.

In the foliage an immense jackdaw sat looking at Julian, and here and there among the branches glowed countless lights as if all the stars in the firmament had rained down into the forest. They were the eyes of animals, wild cats, squirrels, owls, parrots, monkeys.

Julian shot his arrows at them; the feathered arrows landed on the leaves like so many white butterflies. He threw stones; the stones fell without hitting anything. Fighting mad, he cursed, screamed imprecations, choked with rage.

And all the animals which he had pursued came back, enclosing him in a tight circle, some crouching, others upright. He stayed in the middle, frozen with terror, unable to make the slightest movement. With a supreme effort of will he took a step; the ones which perched in the trees spread their wings, those which trod on the ground moved their limbs; and they all accompanied him.

The hyenas walked in front; the wolf and the boar behind. The bull, on his right, swayed its head; and on his left, the snake wriggled through the grass, while the panther, arching its back, advanced with long, velvety strides. He went as slowly as possible lest he should anger them; and he saw emerging from the depths of the undergrowth porcupines, foxes, vipers, jackals, and bears.

Julian began to run; they ran. The snake hissed, the stinking beasts* slobbered, the boar rubbed its tusks against his heels, the wolf rasped his palms with its hairy muzzle. The monkeys pulled faces as they pinched him, the marten rolled over his feet. A bear knocked off his hat with a backward flick of its paw; and the panther contemptuously dropped an arrow it was carrying in its mouth.

A mocking irony was evident in their stealthy movements. Watching him with sidelong glances, they seemed to be contemplating some plan of revenge; deafened with the buzzing of the insects, buffeted by the birds' tails, suffocated by the animals' breath, he walked on with arms outstretched and eyes closed like a blind man, without the strength even to cry for mercy.

A cockcrow rang through the air. Others answered; day had broken, and beyond the orange trees he recognized the roof of his palace.

Then at the edge of a field, he saw some red partridges fluttering about in the stubble, three paces away. He undid his cloak and threw it over them like a net. When he took it off to uncover them he found only one, long dead and rotten.

This disappointment made him angrier than all the others. Blood lust possessed him again; failing animals, he would have liked to slaughter men.

He went up the three terraces, broke open the door with his fist; but, at the foot of the stairs, the recollection of his dear wife softened his heart. No doubt she was asleep; he would give her a surprise.

Taking off his sandals, he softly turned the latch and went in.

The leaded lights dimmed the pale gleam of dawn. Julian caught his feet in some clothes lying on the floor; a little further on he bumped into a serving table still laden with dishes. 'She must have had something to eat,' he said to himself; and went on towards the bed, lost in darkness at the far end of the room. When he was beside it, going to kiss his wife, he bent over the pillow on which the two heads rested side by side. Then he felt his lips touch what seemed to be a beard.

He recoiled, thinking he was going mad; but came back close to the bed, and his probing fingers met some long strands of hair. Wanting to make sure that he had been mistaken, he slowly ran his hand again over the pillow. It certainly was a beard, this time, and a man! a man in bed with his wife!

Exploding with uncontrollable rage, he leaped upon them, thrusting with his dagger, stamping, foaming at the mouth, screaming like some wild animal. Then he stopped. The dead bodies, stabbed in the heart, had not even moved. He listened intently to the death rattle coming from the two of them almost as one, and as it began to fade away, another, far off, prolonged it. At first hesitant, this long-drawn-out cry of pain came ever nearer, swelled, became cruel; and terror-struck he recognized the belling of the great black stag.

Turning round, he thought he saw his wife's ghost standing in the doorway with a light in her hand.

The noise of the murder had drawn her. Taking everything in at a glance, she fled in horror, dropping her torch.

He picked it up.

His father and mother lay there before him on their backs, with holes gaping in their chests; and their faces, majestically gentle, seemed to be keeping some eternal secret. Splashes and stains of blood showed starkly against the whiteness of their skin, on the sheets, on the floor, down an ivory crucifix hanging in the alcove. The crimson reflection from the stained-glass window, just then catching the sun, lit up these red patches and scattered others still more plentifully about the room. Julian went towards the two dead bodies telling himself, longing to believe, that it was just not possible, that he was somehow mistaken, that likenesses may occur for which there is no explanation. Finally he stooped slightly to look at the old man from close at hand; and he saw, between the half-closed lids, a lifeless eye which burned him like fire. Then he went round to the other side of the bed, where the other body lay, its white hair veiling part of the face. Julian slipped his fingers under the strands, lifted the head and, holding it at arm's length, gazed at it by the light of the torch in his other hand. Drops oozing from the mattress fell one by one upon the floor.

At the end of the day he appeared before his wife; and in a voice unlike his own, ordered her first of all not to answer him, not to come near him, not even to look at him again; she must, on pain of damnation, follow out all his orders, which were irrevocable.

The funeral would be conducted according to the written instructions which he had left on a prayer-stool in the room where the dead bodies lay. He was leaving her his palace, his vassals, all his property, without retaining even the clothes on his back, or his sandals, which would be found at the head of the stairs.

She had obeyed God's will in furnishing the occasion of his crime, and was to pray for his soul, since he ceased henceforth to exist.

The dead were given a magnificent funeral, in a monastery church three days' journey from the castle. A monk, with his cowl pulled down over his face, followed the cortege, at a distance from everyone else, and no one dared speak to him.

He remained during the Mass prostrated in the middle of the doorway, arms extended and face in the dust.

After the burial, he was seen taking the road which led to the mountains. He turned round several times, and finally disappeared.

III

HE went away, living off what he could beg throughout the world.

He would hold out his hand to horsemen riding along the highway, he would go up to harvesters, bending his knee, or stand motionless at the gates of farmyards; and his face was so sad that no one ever refused him alms.

In a spirit of humility he would tell his story; then everyone would run away, making the sign of the cross. In the villages where he had already been once, as soon as they recognized him they would shut their doors against him, shout threats, throw stones at him. The more charitable would put out a bowl on their windowsill, then close the shutters so that they would not see him.

Rejected everywhere, he kept away from people; and he lived on roots, plants, windfalls and shellfish, which he would seek on the shore.

Sometimes, coming round a hill, he would see laid out before him a jumble of roofs huddled together, with stone steeples, bridges, towers, a maze of dark streets, from which a constant hubbub rose to his ears.

The need to share the existence of others drove him down into the city. But the brutish faces, the din of the different trades, the heedless chatter, chilled his heart. On feast days, when the cathedral's great bell boomed out from first light to bring joy to all, he would watch the townsfolk come out of their houses, then the dancing in the squares, with the beer flowing from the crossroads fountains, and the damask hangings in front of the prince's residence, and at nightfall, looking through ground-floor windows at the long family tables where grandparents held grandchildren on their knees, he would choke with sobs, and go back into the country.

He would gaze with pangs of love at foals in the meadows, birds in their nests, insects on the flowers; all, as he drew near, would run away, hide in terror, quickly fly off.

He sought lonely places. But the wind brought to his ears moans like a death rattle; dewdrops pattering to the ground reminded him of other drops falling so much more heavily. Every evening the sun streaked the clouds with blood; and every night, in his dreams the murder of his parents began all over again.

He made himself a hairshirt with iron spikes. He climbed on his knees every hill with a chapel at its top. But his thoughts were relentless, dimming the splendour of the tabernacles, torturing him through all the mortifications of his penance.

He did not rebel against God who had inflicted such a deed upon him, and yet he was in despair at the fact that he had been able to do it.

His own body filled him with such revulsion that, in the hope of winning freedom from it, he exposed himself to the greatest dangers. He saved the palsied from fires, children from deep chasms. The abyss cast him back, the flames spared him.

Time did not still his suffering. It was becoming intolerable. He resolved to die.

And one day when he found himself beside a spring, leaning over to gauge the depth of the water, there appeared before him an emaciated old man, with a white beard and so piteous a look that Julian was unable to hold back his tears. The other wept too. Without recognizing his own image, Julian vaguely remembered a face rather like it. He cried out—it was his father; and he thought no more of killing himself.

Thus heavily laden with his memories he travelled through many lands; and came by a river which it was dangerous to cross, because of its fierce current and because a great expanse of mud lay on either bank. No one had dared to cross it for a long time.

An old boat, buried by the stern, stuck its prow out of the reeds. On closer inspection Julian discovered a pair of oars; and it occurred to him to devote his life to the service of others.

He began by constructing on the bank a sort of causeway, which would afford direct access to the channel; and he tore his nails shifting huge boulders, resting them against his belly to carry them; he slipped in the mud, sank into it, all but perished a number of times.

Next he repaired the boat with timber from wrecks, and made himself a shack out of clay and tree trunks.

As the ferry became known, travellers appeared. They would hail him from the other side, waving flags; Julian would quickly jump into his boat. It was very heavy; and people would overload it with all kinds of baggage and burden, not to mention pack animals which, rearing with fright, made it still more unwieldy. He asked nothing for his pains; some gave him scraps of food from their wallets or clothes so worn that they did not want them any more. The rough ones would bawl out blasphemies. Julian gently reproved them, and they would reply with insults. He was content just to bless them.

A small table, a stool, a bed of dead leaves and three clay bowls were all the furniture he had. Two holes in the wall served as windows. On one side, as far as the eye could see, stretched barren plains with wan pools lying here and there on their surface, while in front of him the green waters of the great river rolled on. In spring the damp earth smelled of corruption. Then an unruly wind would raise the dust in swirling clouds. It penetrated everywhere, made the water muddy, gritted against his teeth. A little later came clouds of mosquitoes, buzzing and stinging incessantly day and night. Then came dreadful frosts, which made everything as stiff as stone, and brought on a violent craving for meat.

Months would pass without Julian seeing a soul. He would often close his eyes, trying in memory to return to his youth—and a castle courtyard would appear, with greyhounds on a terrace, servants in the armoury and, in an arbour of vine-branches, a fair-haired youth between an old man clad in furs and a lady with a tall hennin. Suddenly the two corpses were there instead. He would fling himself face down on his bed, and weep as he repeated:

'Oh! Poor father! Poor mother! Poor mother!' And when he finally dozed off, even in sleep the funereal visions would go on and on.

One night when he was asleep he thought he heard someone calling him. He listened intently, but could only make out the roaring of the water.

But the same voice said again: 'Julian!'

It came from the other side, which seemed extraordinary, considering the width of the river.

The call came a third time: 'Julian!'

And the voice rang out loud and clear like a church bell.

Lighting his lantern, he left his hut. A howling gale filled the night. All lay deep in darkness, rent here and there by the white caps of the tossing waves.

After a moment's hesitation, Julian cast off the moorings. The water at once fell calm, the boat glided over it and reached the other bank, where a man stood waiting.

He was wrapped in a tattered sheet, his face like a plaster mask and his eyes glowing redder than live coals. As Julian brought the lantern closer, he saw that the man was covered with a hideous leprosy; yet there was something regal and majestic in his bearing.

As soon as he stepped into the boat it sank down wondrously deep beneath his crushing weight; it came up again with a jerk, and Julian began to row.

With each stroke of the oars, the surge of the waves lifted the boat up by the bows. The water, blacker than ink, raged by on either side of the hull. It scooped out great troughs, piled up mountainously, and the boat leaped up, then plunged down into the depths, where it whirled round, tossed by the wind.

Julian bent his body, stretched his arms to the full, and bracing himself with his feet, threw himself back with a twist of the hips for greater thrust. Hailstones lashed his hands, rain ran down his back, the violence of the gale took his breath away; he stopped. Then the boat drifted helplessly away. But realizing that a momentous issue was at stake, a command not to be disobeyed, he took up the oars again; and the thud of the rowlocks cut through the clamour of the storm.

The little lantern burned in front of him. Birds fluttering by hid it now and then. But all the time he saw the eyes of the Leper, who stood in the stern, immobile as a pillar.

And that lasted a long time, a very long time!

When they reached the hut, Julian closed the door; and saw him sitting on the stool. The kind of shroud which covered him had fallen down to his waist; his shoulders, his chest, his skinny arms were barely visible beneath patches of scaly pustules. Huge wrinkles furrowed his brow. Like a skeleton, he had two holes in place of a nose; and through his blue-tinged lips came a nauseous breath as thick as fog.

'I am hungry!' he said.

Julian gave him what he had, an old hunk of bacon and some crusts of black bread.

When he had devoured this the table, the bowl, and the knife handle bore the same spots as were to be seen on his body.

Julian went to fetch his pitcher; and as he picked it up, there came from it a smell which made his heart and nostrils dilate. It was wine; what a lucky find! But the Leper stretched out his arm, and drained the pitcher with one gulp.

Then he said: 'I am cold!'

Julian took the candle and set light to a bundle of bracken in the middle of the hut.

The Leper came to warm himself by it; and squatting on his heels, he shivered in every limb, grew weaker; his eyes no longer shone, his sores were running, and in the faintest whisper he murmured:

'Your bed!'

Julian gently helped him to drag himself on to it, and even spread over him, as a covering, the canvas from his boat.

The Leper kept groaning, the corners of his mouth drew back to reveal his teeth, his chest shook as his death rattle became ever more rapid and with each breath he took, his belly sank to meet his backbone.

Then he closed his eyes.

'My bones are like ice! Come beside me!'

And Julian moved aside the canvas and lay down on the dead leaves next to him, side by side.

The Leper turned his head.

'Take off your clothes, so that I can have the warmth of your body!'

Julian undressed; then, naked as the day he was born, settled back on the bed; and he felt against his thigh the Leper's skin, colder than a snake and rough as a file.

He tried to hearten him, and the other answered with gasps:

'Oh! I am going to die! Come closer, warm me! Not just with your hands! No, with your whole body!'

Julian lay full length on top of him, mouth to mouth, chest to chest.

Then the Leper embraced him; and his eyes suddenly shone as bright as stars; his hair streamed out like the rays of the sun;

the breath from his nostrils was as sweet as roses; a cloud of incense rose from the hearth, the waters sang. Meanwhile delights in abundance, a superhuman joy came flooding into the soul of Julian, who lay in a swoon; and the one whose arms still clasped him tight grew larger, larger, until his head and his feet touched the walls of the hut. The roof flew off, the firmament unfolded—and Julian rose up into the blue of space, face to face with Our Lord Jesus, who bore him off to heaven.

And that is the story of Saint Julian the Hospitaller, more or less as it can be found in the stained-glass window*of a church in my part of the world.

Herodias

THE citadel of Machaerus* stood to the east of the Dead Sea
on a conical peak of basalt. Four deep valleys surrounded it,
one on each side, one in front, one behind. Houses crowded
up against its base within the circle of a wall which rose and
fell with the uneven contours of the ground; and a zigzag
path slashed through the rock connected the town with the
fortress, whose walls rose a hundred and twenty cubits high,
with numerous angles, crenellated edges and, here and there,
towers set like florets on this stone crown, suspended over
the abyss.

Inside was a palace adorned with porticoes, and on top lay
a terrace, enclosed with a balustrade of sycamore-wood, on
which were set poles for a velarium.*

One morning, before daybreak, the Tetrarch Herod-
Antipas came to lean on the balustrade and look round.

The mountains immediately beneath him were beginning
to reveal their crests, while their main bulk, extending down
into the abyss, still lay in darkness. A veil of mist floated in
the air, then through a break the outlines of the Dead Sea
appeared. Dawn rising behind Machaerus suffused a rosy
glow. Soon it lit up the sandy shore, the hills, the desert, and,
further off, the mountains of Judaea with their rugged grey
slopes. Engeddi in the middle scored a dark line across the
landscape; Hebron, further back, formed a rounded dome;
Eshcol had pomegranate trees, Sorek vineyards, Carmel*
fields of sesame; and the enormous cube of the Antonia
tower dominated Jerusalem. The Tetrarch looked away
to the right to gaze at the palm trees of Jericho;* and he
thought of the other towns of his Galilee: Capernaum,
Endor, Nazareth, Tiberias, to which he might perhaps

never again return. Meanwhile the Jordan flowed over the arid plain, which in its total whiteness dazzled like a sheet of snow. The lake now seemed to be made of lapis-lazuli; and at its most southerly tip, towards the Yemen,* Antipas recognized what he feared to see. Brown tents were scattered about, men with spears moved about among the horses and dying fires flashed and sparkled on the ground.

They were the troops of the Arabian king, whose daughter he had put away so that he could take Herodias, the wife of one of his brothers, who lived in Italy with no pretensions to power.

Antipas was waiting for help from the Romans; but Vitellius, governor of Syria, was so slow to appear that he was devoured by anxiety.

Agrippa, no doubt, had brought him into disrepute with the Emperor? Philip, his third brother, ruler of Batanea, was arming in secret. The Jews had had enough of his idolatrous ways, everyone else of his rule. As a result he was hesitating between two plans: soothing the Arabs or concluding an alliance with the Parthians; and on the pretext of celebrating his birthday, he had invited to a great feast on that very day the leaders of his troops, the stewards of his estates, and the notables of Galilee.

He keenly scrutinized all the roads. They were empty. Eagles flew above his head; along the ramparts the soldiers slept against the walls; nothing stirred in the castle.

Suddenly a distant voice, as though issuing from the bowels of the earth, made the Tetrarch turn pale. He bent down to listen; it had fallen silent. It began again; he clapped his hands and cried:

'Mannaei! Mannaei!'

A man appeared, naked to the waist like the masseurs at the baths. He was very tall, old, rawboned, and on his thigh he bore a cutlass in a bronze scabbard. His hair, swept up with a comb, accentuated the height of his forehead. His

eyes were dull with sleep, but his teeth gleamed bright and
his toes sprang nimbly over the paving; his whole body
was as agile as a monkey's and his features as impassive as
a mummy's.

'Where is he?' asked the Tetrarch.

Mannaei replied, pointing his thumb at something behind
them:

'There! still there!'

'I thought I heard him!'

And Antipas, taking a deep breath, enquired about
Iaokanann, the same whom the Latins call Saint John the
Baptist. Had any more been seen of the two men who, as a
favour, had been allowed into his dungeon the other month,
and had anyone learned subsequently what they had come
for?

Mannaei answered:

'They exchanged mysterious words with him, like robbers
meeting at dusk at crossroads. Then they went off towards
Upper Galilee, promising to bring back great news.'

Antipas bowed his head; then, looking terror-struck:

'Guard him! Guard him! Admit no one! Close the door
securely! Cover up the pit! No one must even suspect that
he is alive!'

Without waiting for such orders Mannaei was already
carrying them out; for Iaokanann was a Jew, and, like all
Samaritans,* he loathed the Jews.

Their temple at Gerizim, appointed by Moses to be the
centre of Israel, had ceased to exist since King Hyrcan;
and the one in Jerusalem infuriated them as a permanent
outrage and injustice. Mannaei had managed to get inside it
to defile the altar with the bones of the dead. His less speedy
companions had been beheaded.

He caught sight of the temple in the gap between two
hills. Its walls of white marble and the gold plates on
the roof glistened in the sun. It was like a luminous

mountain, something superhuman, crushing everything with its opulence and its pride.

Then he stretched out his arms towards Zion; standing straight, with head thrown back and fists clenched, he put a curse on it, believing in the effective power of the words.

Antipas listened, apparently not shocked.

The Samaritan went on:

'At times he is restless, he wants to escape, hopes for release. At other times he is quiet, like a sick animal, or I see him walking about in the dark, repeating to himself: "What does it matter? For him to increase, I must decrease."'*

Antipas and Mannaei looked at each other. But the Tetrarch was weary with reflection.

All these mountains around him, rising in tiers like great petrified waves, the dark chasms in the side of the cliffs, the vastness of the blue sky, the harsh glare of the sunlight, the depth of the abysses troubled him; and he was filled with despondency at the sight of the wilderness, with its chaotic landscape calling to mind ruined amphitheatres and palaces. The hot wind smelling of sulphur seemed to bring with it exhalations from the cursed cities,* now buried below shore level beneath the weight of the waters. These signs of undying wrath filled his mind with dread; he stayed, both elbows resting on the balustrade, gazing out, head in hands. Someone had touched him. Herodias stood before him.

She was swathed in a light purple cymar* that came down to her sandals. She had left her room in such a hurry that she wore neither necklace nor earrings; a plait of her black hair fell over one arm, its end plunging between her breasts. Her flaring nostrils quivered; her face lit up with triumphant joy; she shook the Tetrarch as she cried loudly:

'Caesar is our friend! Agrippa is in prison!'

'Who told you so?'

'I know!'

She added, 'It is because he wished that the empire might pass to Caius!'*

While living off their charity he had intrigued for the title of king, to which they aspired as much as he. But for the future they had nothing more to fear!—'Tiberius' dungeons do not open readily, and sometimes survival there is far from sure!'

Antipas understood her, and although she was Agrippa's sister, her appalling intention seemed to him to be justified. Such murders were in the nature of things, inevitable in royal houses. In Herod's family they were now too numerous to count.

Then she revealed what measures she had taken: clients bribed, letters disclosed, spies at every door, and how she had managed to seduce Eutychus the informer. 'I did not count the cost! For your sake have I not done more? . . . I gave up my daughter!'*

After her divorce she had left the child in Rome, expecting to have others by the Tetrarch. She never spoke of her. He wondered what had caused this sudden rush of affection.

The velarium had been unfurled, and large cushions had been swiftly placed beside them. Herodias sank down on them, in tears, turning her back on him. Then she brushed her hand over her eyes, said that she did not want to think about it any more, that she was quite happy; and she reminded him of their conversations there, in the Atrium, their meetings in the baths, their walks along the Sacred Way, and their evenings in the great villas, with the fountains plashing, beneath arches of flowers, with the Roman countryside before them. She looked at him as she used to, rubbing up against his chest, fondling him. He pushed her away. The love she was trying to revive was so far away, now! And all his misfortunes originated from it; for the war had been going on for nearly twelve years now. It had aged the Tetrarch. His shoulders were stooped beneath his dark, purple-bordered toga; his white hair mingled with his beard, and the sun striking through the awning lit up his gloomy brow. Herodias' too was furrowed; and they confronted each other with hostile stares.

The mountain paths began to show signs of life. Herdsmen goaded on their oxen, children tugged donkeys along, grooms led horses. Those who were coming down the heights behind Machaerus disappeared behind the castle; others were climbing up the ravine opposite, and once they arrived in the town were unloading their baggage in its courtyards. These were the Tetrarch's suppliers, and servants preceding his guests.

But at the end of the terrace, to the left, appeared an Essene* in a white robe, barefoot, with a stoical expression. Mannaei rushed at him from the right, brandishing his cutlass.

Herodias cried out: 'Kill him!'

'Stop!' said the Tetrarch.

He stopped still; so did the other.

Then they withdrew, each down a different staircase, moving backwards, never losing sight of each other.

'I know him!' said Herodias, 'His name is Phanuel, and he wants to see Iaokanann, since you have been shortsighted enough to keep him alive!'

Antipas objected; one day he might be useful. His attacks on Jerusalem were winning over to their side the rest of the Jews.

'No!' she replied, 'They will accept any master and are incapable of forming a nation!' As for the one who was stirring up the people with hopes preserved ever since the time of Nehemiah,* the best policy was to do away with him.

There was no hurry, according to the Tetrarch. 'Iaokanann dangerous? Come now!' He pretended to laugh at the idea.

'Be quiet!' And she told again of her humiliation, one day when she was going down to Gilead for the balsam harvest. 'There were people on the river bank putting their clothes on again. On a mound to one side, a man was speaking. He wore a camel skin around his loins, and his head was like the head of a lion. As soon as he saw me he spat out at me all the curses of the prophets. His eyes flashed; his voice roared; he raised his arms as though to pull down a thunderbolt. There was no way to escape. My chariot wheels were in sand up to the axles; and I moved off slowly, sheltering beneath my cloak, chilled by these insults pouring down like rain in a storm.'

Iaokanann was making her life impossible. When he had been seized and tied up, the soldiers were ordered to stab him if he offered resistance; he had taken it quietly. Snakes had been put into his prison cell; they had died.

The futility of these intended traps annoyed Herodias. Besides, why did he campaign against her? What were his motives? The words he spoke, cried out to crowds of people, had been widely broadcast and still circulated; she heard them everywhere, they filled the air. Faced with legions she would have fought bravely, but this force, more destructive than the sword, and quite intangible, left her stunned; and she paced the terrace, pale with anger, lost for words to describe why she was choking with rage.

She was wondering too whether the Tetrarch, yielding to public opinion, might not decide to put her away. Then all would be lost! Since she was a child she had nourished dreams of a great empire. It was in furtherance of that ambition that she had left her first husband and joined this one, who had made a fool of her, as she now thought.

'A fine lot of support I found when I married into your family!'

'It's as good as yours!' the Tetrarch simply said.

Herodias felt the ancestral blood* of priests and kings boil in her veins.

'But your grandfather was a sweeper in the temple of Askalom! The others were just a horde of shepherds, bandits, caravan-drivers, paying tribute to Judah since David's time! All my ancestors beat yours! The first of the Maccabees chased you out of Hebron, Hyrcan forced circumcision on you!' Then venting the contempt of the patrician for the plebeian, the hatred of Jacob against Edom, she reproached him for his indifference to insult, his softness towards the Pharisees who were betraying him, his cowardice towards the people who loathed her. 'You are just like them, admit it! And you miss that Arab girl dancing round her lumps of stone! Take her back! Go off and live with her in her canvas home! Gobble up the bread she bakes under the ashes! Gulp the curdled milk from her ewes! Kiss her blue-painted cheeks! And forget me!'

The Tetrarch was not listening any more. He was looking at the flat roof of a house, where there was a young girl, and an old woman holding a sunshade with a handle made from a reed as long as an anglers rod. In the middle of a carpet a huge travelling hamper stood open. Belts, veils and gold-wrought pendants spilled out of it in confusion. The girl periodically bent over these objects and shook them in the air. She was dressed like the Roman women in a pleated tunic and a peplum with emerald tassels; blue bands held her hair in place, but it must have been too heavy, for from time to time she put her hand up to it. The shadow of the sunshade moved above her, partly hiding her. Two or three times Antipas caught sight of her delicate neck, the slant of an eye, the corner of a small mouth. But he could see, from her waist to her neck, her whole torso bending and straightening again as flexibly as a spring. He watched out for this movement to be repeated, and his breath came faster; his eyes began to blaze. Herodias observed him.

He asked: 'Who is that?'

She replied that she did not know, and left, suddenly pacified.

Awaiting the Tetrarch under the porticoes were some Galileans, his chief scribe, the head man of his pastures, the overseer of the saltworks, and a Babylonian Jew, who commanded his horsemen. They all hailed him with acclamation. Then he disappeared in the direction of the inner chambers.

Phanuel suddenly appeared at the bend of a corridor.

'Oh, you again? You have come to see Iaokanann, I suppose?'

'And to see you! I have something very important to tell you.'

And, staying with Antipas, he followed behind him into a dimly lit room.

Light came in through a grille, running along beneath the cornice. The walls were painted dark red, almost black. At the far end stretched an ebony bed, with ox-hide straps. A golden shield above it shone like a sun.

Antipas went right across the room and lay down on the bed.

Phanuel remained standing. He raised his arm, and in the attitude of one inspired:

'The Almighty sends out one of his sons from time to time. Iaokanann is such a one. If you treat him badly you will be punished.'

'It is he who is persecuting me!' cried Antipas. 'He wanted me to do something impossible. Since then he has been tormenting me. And I was not harsh to begin with! He has even sent out from Machaerus men who are throwing my province into turmoil. Woe on him! Since he attacks me, I defend myself!'

'He is too violent in his anger,' replied Phanuel. 'No matter! He must be freed.'

'You don't release wild animals!' said the Tetrarch.

The Essene answered:

'Don't worry! He'll go to the Arabs, the Gauls, the Scythians. His work must reach to the ends of the earth!'

Antipas seemed to be lost in a vision.

'His power is great! . . . Despite myself I like him!'

'So, he goes free?'

The Tetrarch shook his head. He was afraid of Herodias, of Mannaei, of the unknown.

Phanuel tried to talk him round, citing as a guarantee for his plans the Essenes' past submission to the kings. People respected these poor men, who could not be cowed by punishment, who dressed in coarse linen and read the future in the stars.

Antipas recalled something that had been said shortly before.

'What is this thing that you told me was so important?'

A negro came in. His body was white with dust. He gasped for breath and could only say:

'Vitellius!'

'What? Is he on his way?'

'I have seen him. He'll be here within three hours!'

The door curtains in the corridors were shaken as though by the wind. A tumult filled the castle, the noise of people running, furniture being dragged about, silverware crashing down; and from the topmost towers trumpets sounded to warn the scattered slaves.

II

THE ramparts were thick with people when Vitellius entered the courtyard. He leaned on the arm of his interpreter, followed by a great red litter decorated with plumes and mirrors; he wore the toga, the broad purple stripe of the laticlave* and the boots of a consul, and he was escorted by lictors.

They stacked their twelve fasces—that is, a bundle of rods strapped together with an axe in the middle—against the gate. Whereupon all trembled at the majesty of the Roman people.

The litter, which it took eight men to handle, stopped. Out stepped a youth, pot-bellied and pimply, his fingers all decked with pearls. He was offered a goblet full of spiced wine. He drank it and demanded another.

The Tetrarch had fallen at the Proconsul's knees, regretting, as he said, that he had not had earlier notice of the favour of his presence. Otherwise he would have ordered all such measures to be taken along their route as befitted members of the Vitellius family. They were descended from the goddess Vitellia. A road leading from the Janiculum to the sea still bore their name. Countless members of the family had held office as questors or consuls; as for Lucius, now his guest, thanks were due to him as conqueror of the Clites* and father of this young Aulus,* who seemed to be returning to his own domain, since the East was the home of the gods. These hyperboles were couched in Latin. Vitellius received them impassively.

He replied that Herod the Great* was enough to ensure the glory of a nation. The Athenians had made him director of the Olympic games. He had built temples in honour of Augustus; he had been patient, ingenious, fearsome, and always loyal to the Caesars.

Between the columns with their bronze capitals Herodias could be seen approaching with the air of an empress, in the midst of women and eunuchs holding silver-gilt trays on which burned perfumes.

The Proconsul took three steps forward to meet her, and bowed his head in greeting:

'How fortunate', she cried, 'that in future Agrippa, Tiberius' enemy, will be unable to do any harm!'

He did not know the event to which she referred; she struck him as being dangerous. As Antipas was swearing that he would do anything for the Emperor, Vitellius added: 'Even to the detriment of others?'

Vitellius had extracted hostages from the Parthian king, but the Emperor now ignored the fact, for Antipas, who had been present at the conference, had immediately despatched the news in order to win credit for himself. Whence Vitellius' hatred of Antipas and his delay in providing assistance.

The Tetrarch stammered something, but Aulus said with a laugh:

'Don't worry! I'll protect you!'

The Proconsul pretended not to have heard. The father's fortune depended on the son's defilement; and this flower from the mire of Capri* earned him such important benefits that he showed it every consideration, while remaining wary, because it was poisonous.

A commotion arose under the gateway. A file of white mules was being led in, ridden by men in priestly garb. They were Sadducees and Pharisees, driven to Machaerus by the same ambition, the former seeking to obtain the office of High Priest,* the others to retain it. Their faces were sombre, particularly those of the Pharisees, enemies of Rome and of the Tetrarch. The skirts of their tunics impeded them in the crush, and their tiaras* sat unsteadily on their heads above the strips of parchment inscribed with texts from the Scriptures.

Almost at the same time the soldiers of the advance guard arrived. They had put their shields in sacks as a protection against the dust; behind them came Marcellus, the Proconsul's lieutenant, with some publicans, gripping wooden tablets under their arms.

Antipas introduced the principal members of his entourage: Tolmai, Kanthera, Sehon, Ammonius of Alexandria, who bought asphalt for him, Naaman, captain of his light infantry, Iakim the Babylonian.

Vitellius had noticed Mannaei:

'Who is that one over there?'

The Tetrarch conveyed with a gesture that he was the executioner.

Then he presented the Sadducees.

Jonathan, a little man with a relaxed manner, who spoke Greek, begged their master to honour them with a visit to Jerusalem. He would probably go there, he said.

Eleazar, who had a hooked nose and a long beard, laid claim on behalf of the Pharisees to the High Priest's mantle, kept by the civil authority in the Antonia tower. .

Then the Galileans denounced Pontius Pilate.* When some madman was looking for David's gold vessels in a cave, Pilate had killed some of the local people; they were all speaking at once, Mannaei more vehemently than the others. Vitellius assured them that the criminals would be punished.

Shouting broke out in front of a portico where the soldiers had hung up their shields. The covers had been undone, and Caesar's image could be seen on the bosses. For the Jews that was an act of idolatry. Antipas harangued them, while Vitellius, on a raised seat in the colonnade, was amazed at their fury. Tiberius had been right to send four hundred of them off into exile on Sardinia. But in their own land they were strong, and he ordered the shields to be taken down.

Then they surrounded the Proconsul, begging for wrongs to be righted, for privileges, for alms. Clothes were torn, people crushed, and, to clear a space, slaves with staves hit out right and left. Those nearest the gate went down the path, others came up; they surged back; two streams clashed in this heaving mass of humanity, compressed by the enclosing walls.

Vitellius asked why there was such a crowd. Antipas explained that they had come for his birthday feast; and he showed several of his people leaning over the battlements, hauling up huge baskets of meat, fruit, vegetables, antelopes and storks, large blue fish, grapes, water-melons, pyramids of pomegranates. Aulus could stand it no longer. He rushed off to the kitchens, carried away by a gluttony which was to cause universal amazement.

As he passed by a cellar he saw some pots like breastplates; Vitellius came to look at them, and demanded that the underground chambers of the fortress should be opened for him.

They were hewn out of the rock into high vaults, with pillars spaced at intervals. The first contained old armour; but the second was crammed with pikes, their points all sticking out from bunches of feathers. The third seemed to be lined with rush-mats, so straight were the slender arrows stacked side by side. Scimitar blades covered the walls of the fourth. In the middle of the fifth room rows of crested helmets formed up like a regiment of red serpents. There was nothing to be seen in the sixth but quivers; in the seventh, greaves; in the eighth, armbands; in those which followed, pitchforks, climbing irons, scaling ladders, ropes, even booms for catapults, even bells for the dromedaries' chest-harness! And as the mountain widened out towards its base, hollowed out inside like a beehive, below these chambers lay others more numerous, and at still greater depths.

Vitellius, Phineas, his interpreter, and Sisenna, chief of the publicans, went through by the light of torches, carried by three eunuchs.

In the shadows could be discerned hideous objects invented by the barbarians: nail-studded clubs, poisoned javelins, pincers like crocodile jaws; in short, the Tetrarch possessed in Machaerus munitions of war for forty thousand men.

He had collected them in anticipation of an alliance of his enemies. But the Proconsul might believe, or say, that it was for fighting the Romans, and he tried to find explanations.

The munitions were not his; much was for defensive use against brigands; besides, he needed them against the Arabs; or else the whole lot had belonged to his father. And instead of walking behind the Proconsul, he went in front, with rapid steps. Then he stood against the wall, concealing it with his toga by stretching out his arms; but the top of a doorway came higher than his head. Vitellius noticed and wanted to know what was inside.

Only the Babylonian could open it.

'Call the Babylonian!'

They waited for him.

His father had come from the banks of the Euphrates to offer himself, together with five hundred horsemen, to Herod the Great, to defend the eastern frontiers. After the division of the kingdom, Iakim had stayed with Philip and now served Antipas.

He arrived, a bow on his shoulder, a whip in his hand. His crooked legs were tightly laced with cords of many colours. His powerful arms emerged from a sleeveless tunic, a fur cap shaded his features, his beard was curled in ringlets.

At first he seemed not to understand the interpreter. But Vitellius glanced at Antipas, who at once repeated his order. Then Iakim pushed against the door with both hands. It slid into the wall.

A breath of warm air was released from the darkness. A winding path led down; they took it and arrived at the entrance to a cave more extensive than the other underground rooms.

At the far end an archway opened on to the precipice, which defended the citadel on that side. A honeysuckle clung to the roof, its flowers hanging down in the bright sunlight. At ground level a trickle of water murmured.

There were white horses in there, perhaps a hundred of them, eating barley from a shelf level with their mouths. They all had their manes painted blue, their hooves encased in esparto-grass protectors, and the hair between their ears puffed out in front like a wig. Their very long tails swished gently at their hocks. The Proconsul was speechless with admiration.

They were wonderful animals, supple as serpents, light as birds. They sped off swift as the rider's arrow, bowled men over and bit them in the belly, picked their way through rocks, leaped over abysses, and could keep up their frenzied gallop across the plains all day long; one word would halt them. As soon as Iakim entered they came to him, like sheep when their shepherd appears; and stretching out their necks, they looked at him anxiously with childlike eyes. From force of habit he let out a hoarse, guttural cry, which filled them with delight; they reared up, eager for open spaces, asking to run free.

For fear that Vitellius might confiscate them, Antipas had imprisoned them in this place, kept specially for the animals in case of siege.

'These stables are no good,' said the Proconsul, 'and you risk losing the animals! Take the inventory, Sisenna!'

The publican took a tablet from his belt, counted the horses and wrote them down.

The agents of the fiscal companies would bribe the governors in order to plunder the provinces. This one sniffed around everywhere, with his ferret's snout and blinking eyes.

At length they went back up to the courtyard.

Round bronze lids set in the middle of the flagstones here and there were covers for the cisterns. The publican noticed one, bigger than the others, which sounded different when trodden on. He struck all of them in turn, then stamped his feet as he shouted:

'I've found it! I've found it! Here is Herod's* treasure!'

The search for his treasure was an obsession with the Romans.

It did not exist, swore the Tetrarch.

All the same, what was down there?

'Nothing! A man, a prisoner.'

'Let's see him!' said Vitellius.

The Tetrarch did not obey; the Jews would learn his secret. His reluctance to open the lid made Vitellius lose patience.

'Break it in!' he cried to the lictors.

Mannaei had guessed what they were about. Seeing an axe, he thought they were going to behead Iaokanann, and he stopped the lictor at the first blow on the plate, fitted between it and the paving a kind of hook, then straightening his long, skinny arms, gently raised it. It crashed over, and all admired the old man's strength. Under the wood-lined lid lay a trapdoor of the same size. A blow of his fist, and its two panels opened out; then a hole came into view, an enormous pit, round which ran a flight of steps with no handrail; and those who were leaning over the edge could see something indistinct and frightening.

A human being lay on the ground, his long hair mingling with the animal skin he wore on his back. He stood up. His forehead touched a horizontally fixed grating; and from time to time he would disappear into the depths of his den.

The sun flashing on the tips of the tiaras and the hilts of the swords made the flagstones unbearably hot; and doves, flying out from the friezes, wheeled above the courtyard. It was the time when Mannaei usually threw them grain. He stayed squatting before the Tetrarch, who stood by Vitellius. The Galileans, the priests, the soldiers, formed a circle behind; all were silent, dreading what was going to happen.

First came a great sigh, uttered in cavernous tones.

Herodias heard it at the other end of the palace. Unable to resist the spell, she went through the throng, and, with one hand on Mannaei's shoulder, bent forward to listen.

The voice rose:

'Woe unto you, * Pharisees and Sadducees, generation of vipers, swollen wineskins, tinkling cymbals!'

They had recognized Iaokanann. His name went round the crowd. Others ran up.

'Woe unto you, oh people! and unto the traitors of Judah, the winebibbers of Ephraim, those who dwell in the fat valley, and reel about with the fumes of their wine!

'May they run to waste like trickling water, like the snail that melts as it crawls, like the untimely birth of a woman that never sees the sun.

'You, Moab, will have to seek refuge in the cypress trees like the sparrows, in caves like the hyrax.* The gates of the fortresses will be smashed more easily than nutshells, the walls will crumble, the towns will burn; and the scourge of the Eternal One shall not cease. He will stir your limbs round in your blood like wool in a dyer's vat. He will rend you like a new harrow; he will scatter all the pieces of your flesh over the mountains!'

What conqueror was he talking about? Was it Vitellius? Only the Romans could effect such slaughter. People could be heard complaining: 'Enough! enough! Make him stop!'

He continued, more loudly:

'Beside the corpses of their mothers little children will crawl over the ashes. At night men will go to look for bread among the ruins, risking the sword. The jackals will snatch at bones in the public places, where old men were wont to talk in the evenings. Your virgins, swallowing their tears, will play the cithar at the stranger's feast, and your bravest sons will stoop, their backs rubbed raw by loads too heavy to be borne!'

The people recalled the days of their exile, all the disasters in their history. These were the words of the prophets of old. Iaokanann delivered them like great blows, one after another.

But then the voice became gentle, harmonious, musical. He foretold liberation, radiance in the heavens, the newborn child putting his arm into the dragon's lair, gold in place of clay, the desert blooming like a rose: 'What is now worth sixty kiccars* will not cost an obole. Fountains of milk will spring from the rock; men will sleep in the winepresses with full bellies. When will you come, you in whom I hope? All the peoples kneel in expectation; your kingdom will be eternal, Son of David!'

The Tetrarch recoiled in outrage, seeing the existence of a Son of David* as a threat to himself.

Iaokanann inveighed against him for his royal title:

'There is no other king than the Eternal One!'—and for his gardens, his statues, his ivory furniture, just like the ungodly Ahab!*

Antipas broke the string of the seal hanging on his chest, and threw it into the pit, commanding him to be silent.

The voice answered:

'I will cry out like a bear, like a wild ass, like a woman in travail!'

'You are already being punished for your incest.* God has afflicted you with the barrenness of a mule!'

This provoked laughter, rippling like the waves.

Vitellius persisted in staying. The interpreter repeated impassively in the Roman tongue all the insults that Iaokanann was bellowing in his own. The Tetrarch and Herodias were constrained to suffer them twice over. He was breathing heavily, while she watched the bottom of the pit with open mouth.

The fearful man threw back his head, gripped the bars and stuck his face up against them, looking like a bush with two live coals glowing in its midst.

'Ah! It is you, Jezebel!'

'You won his heart with the tapping of your shoe. You whinnied like a mare. You set your bed up on the mountains to offer your sacrifice.'

'The Lord will tear off your earrings, your purple robes, your linen veils, the bracelets on your arms, the rings on your toes, the little golden crescents dangling on your forehead, your silver mirrors, your ostrich feather fans, the mother-of-pearl chopines* that make you taller, the diamonds you flaunt so proudly, your scented hair, your painted nails, all the devices of your self-indulgence; and there will not be stones enough to cast at the adulteress!'

She looked round for some support. The Pharisees hypocritically lowered their eyes. The Sadducees averted their heads, for fear of offending the Proconsul. Antipas looked as though he were at his last gasp.

The voice grew louder, swelled forth, rolled and crashed like thunder, and, repeated in the echo reverberating from the mountain, struck Machaerus with one peal after another.

'Lie in the dust, daughter of Babylon! Grind the meal! Undo your girdle, take off your shoe, pull up your skirts, pass across the rivers! Your shame will be laid bare, your dishonour will be seen! Your teeth will break with weeping! The Eternal One abhors the stench of your crimes! Be cursed! cursed! Die like a dog!'

The trapdoor closed, the lid fell back. Mannaei wanted to strangle Iaokanann.

Herodias disappeared. The Pharisees were scandalized. Antipas, in their midst, was justifying his conduct.

'No doubt', Eleazar rejoined, 'a man should marry his brother's wife, but Herodias was not a widow, and moreover she had a child. That is what constituted the offence.'

'Not so! not so!' objected Jonathan the Sadducee. 'The

Law condemns such marriages, without absolutely pro-
scribing them.'

'No matter! I am being most unfairly treated!' said
Antipas. 'After all Absalom slept with his father's wives,
Judah with his daughter-in-law, Amnon with his sister, Lot*
with his daughters.'

Aulus, who had been away sleeping, reappeared at that
moment. When he had had the affair explained to him, he
took the Tetrarch's part. No one should bother with such
nonsense; and he laughed loudly at the priests' disapproval
and Iaokanann's rage.

Herodias, in the middle of the terrace, turned towards
him.

'You are wrong, my lord! He is ordering the people to
withhold their taxes.'

'Is that true?' asked the Publican at once.

Most people answered in the affirmative. The Tetrarch
confirmed the fact.

Vitellius thought the prisoner might escape; and as
Antipas seemed to him to be behaving suspiciously, he
posted sentries at the gates, along the walls and in the
courtyard.

Then he made for his quarters. The deputations of the
priests accompanied him.

Without raising the question of the High Priesthood, each
side voiced its grievances.

They were all pestering him. He dismissed them.

Jonathan was leaving when he saw Antipas in an embrasure, talking to a long-haired man in a white robe, an
Essene, and he regretted having supported him.

One reflection had consoled the Tetrarch. Iaokanann was
no longer his concern; the Romans had taken charge of him.
What a relief! At that moment Phanuel was walking along
the ramparts.

He called him over, and, indicating the soldiers, said:

'They are stronger than I! I cannot set him free! It is not my fault.'

The courtyard was empty. The slaves were resting. Against the background of the red sky, which set the horizon ablaze, even the smallest upright objects stood out in black. Antipas could make out the saltworks at the other end of the Dead Sea, but no longer saw the Arabs' tents. They must have gone away? The moon rose; peace filled his heart.

Phanuel, overcome by grief, stood with his head sunk on his chest. At length he revealed what he had to say.

Since the beginning of the month he had been studying the sky before dawn; the constellation of Perseus being at its zenith, Agalah* was scarcely visible, Algol shone less brightly, Mira-Coeti had disappeared; from this he forecast the death of some notable person, that very night, at Machaerus.

Who? Vitellius was too closely guarded. Iaokanann would not be executed. 'That means me, then!' thought the Tetrarch.

Perhaps the Arabs were going to come back? The Proconsul would find out about his relations with the Parthians! Hired killers from Jerusalem escorted the priests; they had daggers concealed in their clothing; and the Tetrarch was in no doubt as to Phanuel's knowledge of the stars.

He thought of turning to Herodias for help. Yet he hated her. But she would give him courage; and something remained of the enchantment which had once held him in its thrall.

When he went into her room, cinnamon was smoking in a porphyry bowl; powders, unguents, wispy materials, feather-light embroidery, lay scattered about.

He said nothing of Phanuel's prediction, nor of his fear of the Jews and Arabs; she would have charged him with cowardice. He spoke only of the Romans; Vitellius had confided none of his military plans. He presumed him to be a friend of Caius, with whom Agrippa associated; so he faced exile, or perhaps murder.

Herodias, with condescending sympathy, tried to reassure him. At last she took from a little box a strange medal, adorned with Tiberius' profile. That was enough to make the lictors turn pale and drop all charges.

Antipas, moved with gratitude, asked how she had come by it.

'It was given to me,' she replied.

Under a door-hanging opposite a bare arm stretched out, a youthful, charming arm, that could have been fashioned in ivory by Polycleitus.* A little awkwardly, yet with grace, it waved about in search of a tunic forgotten on a stool by the wall.

An old woman gently handed it over through the parted curtain.

Something stirred in the Tetrarch's memory which eluded him.

'Is that slave one of yours?'

'What does it matter to you?' answered Herodias.

III

THE guests filled the banqueting hall.

It had three aisles, like a basilica, separated by columns of sandalwood with bronze capitals covered in sculptures; on them rested two openwork galleries, and a third in gold filigree curved out at the back, facing an enormous open arch at the other end.

Candelabras burning on the tables arranged down the whole length of the nave looked like bouquets of light, among the painted earthenware goblets and copper dishes, the cubes of snow and piles of grapes; but the red blaze of these lights grew gradually dimmer, because the ceiling was so high, and luminous points shone like stars at night through branches. Through the opening of the great bay torches could be seen on the terraces of the houses; for Antipas was giving a feast for his friends, his people and all who had come.

Slaves vigilant as dogs, their feet thrust into felt sandals, moved about carrying platters.

The Proconsul's table stood beneath the gilded gallery on a dais of sycamore boards. Babylonian wall-hangings enclosed it in a kind of tent.

Three ivory couches, one facing and one on each side, were occupied by Vitellius, his son, and Antipas, with the Proconsul by the door, on the left, Aulus on the right, the Tetrarch in the middle.

He wore a heavy black cloak, painted over so thickly as to conceal the weave, his cheeks were made up, his beard trimmed into a fan shape, his hair powdered blue and clasped with a diadem of precious stones. Vitellius had kept on his purple sash, worn diagonally over a linen toga. Aulus wore his robe of violet silk interwoven with silver thread with the sleeves tied together behind his back to keep them out of the way. His hair was dressed in tiered rolls, and a sapphire necklace sparkled on his bosom, plump and white as a woman's. Beside him, sitting cross-legged on a mat, was a very beautiful boy, with a fixed smile. Aulus had seen him in the kitchens, could no longer do without him, and as he found it hard to remember his Chaldaean name, simply called him 'the Asiatic'. From time to time he stretched out on the triclinium.* Then his bare feet dominated the assembly.

On that side were the priests and Antipas' officials, citizens of Jerusalem, leading men from the Greek towns; and, beneath the Proconsul, Marcellus with the publicans, friends of the Tetrarch, the notables of Cana, Ptolemais, Jericho; then, all mixed together, men from the mountains of Lebanon and Herod's old soldiers: a dozen Thracians, a Gaul, two Germans, gazelle hunters, Idumean herdsmen, the sultan of Palmyra, sailors from Eziongaber. Each one had in front of him a cake of soft dough to wipe his fingers on; their arms reached out like vultures' necks to pick out olives, pistachios, almonds. Every face was joyful beneath its garland of flowers.

The Pharisees had refused these wreaths as a Roman impropriety. They shuddered when they were sprinkled with galbanum and incense, a mixture reserved for Temple use.

Aulus rubbed some of it into his armpits, and Antipas promised him a whole load, with three baskets of the genuine balsam which had made Cleopatra covet Palestine.

A captain from his garrison at Tiberias, who had just arrived, stood behind him to report on some unusual events. But his attention was divided between the Proconsul and what was being said at the nearest tables.

The talk was of Iaokanann and suchlike people; Simon of Gitta* washed away sins with fire. A certain Jesus . . .

'The worst of them all!' cried Eleazar. 'What a shameful charlatan!'

Behind the Tetrarch a man stood up, pale as the border of his chlamys.* He stepped off the dais and shouted at the Pharisees:

'That's a lie! Jesus works miracles!'

Antipas wanted to see some.

'You should have brought him along! Tell us about it!'

Then he related how he, Jacob, had gone to Capernaum when his daughter was sick to entreat the Master to heal her. The Master had answered: 'Go home, she is healed!' And he had found her standing at the threshold; she had got up from her sickbed when the palace sundial marked the third hour, the very moment when he approached Jesus.

Certainly, retorted the Pharisees, powerful treatments and herbs do exist! Right here at Machaerus baaras could sometimes be found, the herb that makes you invulnerable; but healing someone without seeing or touching them was quite impossible, unless Jesus used devils.

And Antipas' friends, the chief men of Galilee, joined in, wagging their heads:

'Obviously devils.'

Jacob, standing between their table and that of the priests, maintained a calm and dignified silence.

They challenged him to speak: 'Justify his power!' He bowed his shoulders, and said in a slow, soft voice, as if afraid of himself:

'Do you not know then that he is the Messiah?'

All the priests looked at each other; Vitellius asked for an explanation of the word. His interpreter took a moment before answering.

That is what they called a liberator who would bring them enjoyment of all earthly goods and dominion over all peoples. Some even held that one had to reckon with two of them. The first would be conquered by Gog and Magog, the devils from the North; but the other would destroy the Prince of Evil; for centuries they had been expecting him at any minute.

The priests conferred together, then Eleazar spoke up.

First of all the Messiah would be a son of David, not of a carpenter; he would uphold the Law, this Nazarene attacked it; and a stronger argument still, he was to be preceded by the coming of Elias.

Jacob replied:

'But Elias has come!'

'Elias! Elias!' the crowd repeated, right down to the far end of the hall.

They all saw in their mind's eye an old man with ravens flying overhead, fire from on high kindling an altar, idolatrous priests cast into the torrent, and the women in the galleries thought of the widow of Zarephaph.*

Jacob grew weary with repeating that he knew him! Had seen him! And so had the people!

'His name?'

Then he cried out with all his might:

'Iaokanann!'

Antipas fell back as if struck full in the chest. The Sadducees had pounced on Jacob. Eleazar was holding forth, trying to win a hearing.

When silence had been restored, Antipas adjusted his cloak, and like a judge put questions.

'Since the prophet is dead . . .'

He was interrupted by murmuring. Elias was believed just to have disappeared.

He lost his temper with the crowd, and continued his enquiry:

'You think he has risen from the dead?'

'Why not?' said Jacob.

The Sadducees shrugged their shoulders; Jonathan, opening wide his little eyes, made great efforts to laugh like a clown. What could be more absurd than to claim that a body can have eternal life; and for the Proconsul's benefit he declaimed this line from a contemporary poet:

*Nec crescit, nec post mortem durare videtur.**

But Aulus was leaning over the edge of the triclinium, his forehead bathed in sweat, his face green, fists pressed into his stomach.

The Sadducees pretended to be very upset—next day the High Priesthood was restored to them—Antipas made a great show of despair; Vitellius remained impassive. He was however deeply concerned; with his son he would lose his fortune.

Aulus had hardly finished making himself sick when he wanted to start eating again

'Give me powdered marble, schist* from Naxos, sea-water, anything! Suppose I had a bath!'

He crunched some snow, then, hesitating between a terrine from Commagene and some pink thrushes, he decided on gourds in honey. The Asiatic gazed at him; such a capacity for stuffing food clearly indicated an exceptional being of a superior race.

Bulls' kidneys were served, dormice, nightingales, vine-leaves stuffed with mincemeat; the priests went on discussing resurrection. Ammonius, a pupil of Philo the Platonist, found them stupid, and said as much to some Greeks who were scoffing at oracles. Marcellus and Jacob had joined together. The first was recounting to the other how happy he had felt undergoing Mithraic baptism,* and Jacob was urging him to follow Jesus. Palm and tamarisk wine, wine from Safet and Byblos, flowed from amphoras to bowls, from bowls to drinking cups, from cups to throats; everyone was chattering away, revealing their innermost feelings. Iakim, though a Jew, no longer concealed the fact that he worshipped the planets. A trader from Aphek made the nomads gape in wonder as he listed all the marvels of the temple of Hierapolis; they asked how much it would cost to go on pilgrimage there. Others remained attached to the religion of their birth. An almost sightless German was singing a hymn in honour of the Scandinavian headland* where the gods appear with their faces radiating light; and men from Sichem would not eat any turtle-doves in deference to the dove Azima.

Many of them stood talking in the middle of the hall, their steaming breath mingling with the candle smoke to form a haze in the air. Phanuel went by along the walls. He had just been studying the firmament again, but did not go up to the Tetrarch for fear of being spattered with oil, a major defilement for the Essenes.

Blows resounded against the castle gates.

It was now known that Iaokanann was imprisoned there. Men with torches clambered up the path; a dark mass

swarmed in the ravine; and at intervals they shouted:
'Iaokanann! Iaokanann!'

'What a trouble-maker!' said Jonathan.

'No one will have any money left if he goes on!' added
the Pharisees.

And from all sides came recriminations:

'Protect us!'

'Let's make an end of him!'

'You are giving up religion!'

'Ungodly as the Herods!'

'Less so than you!' retorted Antipas. 'It was my father
who built your temple!'

Then the Pharisees, sons of the outlawed followers of
Matathias,* accused the Tetrarch of his family's crimes.

They had pointed skulls, bristling beards, weak and
puny hands, or else snub noses and great round eyes, like
bulldogs. A dozen of them, scribes and priestly servants,
who fed on the leavings from the sacrifices, pressed forward
as far as the base of the dais, threatening Antipas with
their knives, while he harangued them and the Sadducees
halfheartedly defended him. He saw Mannaei, and signed
to him to leave, while Vitellius' attitude indicated that none
of this had anything to do with him.

The Pharisees, who had stayed on their couches, worked
themselves up into a demoniacal frenzy. They smashed the
plates in front of them. They had been served Maecenas'
favourite dish, wild ass in a stew, an unclean food.

Aulus jeered at them for paying honour to an ass's head,
so it was said, and went on with more gibes about their
aversion to the pig. This was no doubt because that gross
animal had killed their Bacchus; and they were too fond of
wine, for a golden vine had been discovered in the Temple.

The priests did not understand his words. Phineas, a
native of Galilee, refused to translate them. Then his anger
knew no bounds, particularly as the Asiatic had fled in

terror; he was not enjoying the meal, the dishes were too ordinary and crudely prepared! He calmed down when he saw some Syrian ewes' tails, which are just gobbets of fat.

The character of the Jews seemed quite hideous to Vitellius. Their god might well be Moloch,* whose altars he had encountered by the roadside; and he recalled the child sacrifices, and the story of the man whom they fattened up mysteriously. His Latin heart was sickened with disgust at their intolerance, their iconoclastic rage, their brutish stubbornness. The Proconsul wanted to leave. Aulus refused.

With his robe pushed down to his waist, he lay with a heap of food in front of him, too gorged to eat any, but obstinately determined not to leave it.

The people grew more excited. They indulged themselves in plans for independence. They recalled the glory of Israel. All the conquerors had been punished: Antigonus, Crassus, Varus . . .*

'Wretches!' said the Proconsul, for he understood Syriac; his interpreter was only there to give him time to answer.

Antipas quickly pulled out the medal with the Emperor, and trembling as he looked at it, presented it with the image uppermost.

The panels of the golden gallery suddenly swung open; and in a blaze of candles, amid her slaves and festoons of anemones, Herodias appeared; on her head an Assyrian mitre* held fast by a chinstrap; her hair coiled down to spread out over a scarlet peplum, with sleeves slit from top to bottom. With two stone monsters, like those from the Atrides' treasure, standing against the door, she looked like Cybele flanked by her lions; and from the top of the balustrade above Antipas, holding a libation bowl in her hand, she cried:

'Long live Caesar!'

This homage was repeated by Vitellius, Antipas, and the priests.

But coming from the far end of the hall could be heard a buzz of surprise and admiration. A young girl had just come in.

Under a bluish veil which concealed her head and chest, one could make out the arches of her eyes, the chalcedony stones in her ears, the whiteness of her skin. A square of dove-grey silk covered her shoulders, and was fastened at the waist by a jewelled girdle. Her loose black trousers were decorated with mandrake roots, and her little slippers of hummingbird down tapped as she leisurely advanced.

Up on the dais she took off her veil. It was Herodias, as she used to look in her youth. Then she began to dance.

Her feet slipped back and forth, to the rhythm of the flute and a pair of castanets. Her arms curved round in invitation to someone who always eluded her. She pursued him, lighter than a butterfly, like some curious Psyche, like a wandering spirit, and seemed on the point of flying away.

The mournful sound of the gingras* replaced the castanets. Despair had followed hope. Her attitudes expressed sighs, and her whole body such languor that one could not tell whether she was mourning for a god or swooning in his embrace. With eyes half closed, she twisted her waist, made her belly ripple like the swell of the sea, made her breasts quiver, while her expression remained fixed, and her feet never stood still.

Vitellius compared her to Mnester, the mime. Aulus went on being sick. The Tetrarch was lost in reverie, and had forgotten about Herodias. He thought he saw her, over by the Sadducees. The vision receded.

It was no vision. She had arranged instruction for her daughter Salome, far from Machaerus; the Tetrarch would fall in love with her; it had been a good idea. She was sure of that, now!

Then came the wild passion of love demanding satisfaction. She danced like the priestesses of India, like the Nubian women from the cataracts, like the Bacchantes of Lydia. She bent over in every direction, like a flower tossed by the storm. The jewels in her ears leaped about, the silk on her back shimmered, from her arms, her feet, her clothes invisible sparks shot out, firing the men with excitement. A harp sang; the throng responded with applause. Opening wide her legs, without bending her knees, she bowed so low that her chin brushed the floor; and the nomads accustomed to abstinence, the Roman soldiers skilled in debauchery, the avaricious publicans, the old priests soured with controversy, all with flaring nostrils shivered with lust.

Then she whirled round Antipas' table in a frenzy, like the sorceresses' spinning top; and in a voice broken with moans of pleasure he said to her: 'Come! Come!' She went on whirling; the dulcimers beat loud enough to burst, the crowd shouted. But the Tetrarch cried louder still: 'Come! Come! You can have Capernaum! The plain of Tiberias! My citadels! Half my kingdom!'

She sprang up on her hands, heels in the air, crossed the dais in that way, like some great beetle; and suddenly stopped.

Her neck and spine were at right angles; the coloured sheaths that enveloped her legs fell over her shoulders like rainbows on either side of her face, a cubit's length from the ground. Her lips were painted, her eyebrows very black, her eyes almost frightening, and the drops on her forehead looked like a vapour on white marble. She did not speak. They looked at each other.

Someone in the gallery snapped their fingers. She went up, reappeared; and lisping slightly pronounced these words, with a childlike expression:

'I want you to give me on a dish the head ...' She had forgotten the name, but then went on with a smile, 'Iaokanann's head!'

The Tetrarch collapsed, shattered.

He was obliged to keep his word, and the people were waiting. But if the prediction of death were applied to another, perhaps that would avert his own? If Iaokanann really were Elias he could escape death; if he were not, his murder no longer had any significance.

Mannaei stood beside him and understood what he intended.

Vitellius called him over to give him the password for the sentries guarding the dungeon.

It was a relief. In a moment it would all be over!

However Mannaei was certainly taking his time about the job.

He came back, but quite distraught.

He had performed the duties of executioner for forty years. He it was who drowned Aristobulus,* strangled Alexander, burned Matathias alive, beheaded Zozimus, Pappus, Joseph, and Antipater; and he did not dare kill Iaokanann! His teeth chattered, his whole body trembled.

In front of the pit he had seen the Great Angel of the Samaritans, covered all over with eyes, brandishing a huge red sword, jagged as a flame. He had brought along two soldiers who could testify to it.

They had seen nothing, except a Jewish captain, who had rushed at them, and was no longer alive.

Herodias' fury spewed out in a torrent of vulgar and cutting abuse. She broke her nails on the gallery's mesh, and the two carved lions seemed to be biting her shoulders and roaring like her.

Antipas imitated her; the priests, soldiers, Pharisees, all demanded vengeance, and the others were indignant that their pleasure had been delayed.

Mannaei went out, hiding his face.

The guests found the waiting even longer than the first time. They were losing patience.

Suddenly footsteps echoed from the corridors. The suspense became unbearable.

The head came in—and Mannaei held it out at arm's length, by the hair, proud of the applause.

Then he set it on a dish and offered it to Salome.

She nimbly sprang up to the gallery; some minutes later the head was brought down again by the same old woman whom the Tetrarch had noticed that morning on the terrace of a house, and more recently in Herodias' room.

He pulled back to avoid seeing it. Vitellius glanced at it with indifference.

Mannaei came down from the dais, and exhibited the head to the Roman captains, then to all who were eating on that side.

They examined it.

The sharp blade of the weapon, slicing downwards, had caught the jaw. The corners of the mouth were drawn back in convulsion. Blood, already clotted, lay sprinkled on the beard. The closed eyelids were as pale as seashells; and beams from the candelabras all around shone on them.

It came to the priests' table. A Pharisee turned it upside down curiously; and Mannaei, putting it straight again, set it before Aulus, who woke up at that. Through their open lashes the dead eyes and the vacant eyes seemed to be telling each other something.

Then Mannaei presented it to Antipas. Tears flowed down the Tetrarch's cheeks.

The torches flickered out, the guests left; and no one remained in the hall but Antipas, his hands clasping his temples, gazing still at the severed head, while Phanuel, standing in the middle of the great nave, murmured prayers with arms outstretched.

*

Just as the sun was rising, two men, sent out earlier by Iaokanann, arrived with the long hoped-for reply.

They told Phanuel, who was overjoyed.

Then he showed them the mournful object on the dish, amidst the remains of the feast. One of the men said to him:

'Take comfort! He has gone down among the dead to proclaim the Christ!'

Now the Essene understood these words:

'For him to increase, I must decrease.'

And all three, taking Iaokanann's head, went off towards Galilee.

As it was very heavy, they carried it in turn.

Explanatory Notes

A SIMPLE HEART

THE area in which most of the action takes place is the triangle Pont-l'Évêque–Trouville–Honfleur, roughly ten kilometres on each side, and the topography is exact, though of course much has changed since Flaubert's day, particularly along the coast. As for the characters, various models have been proposed for Félicité, of whom the Flaubert family servant, Julie, is the most obvious, but even where names coincide, there is no one-to-one identification for her or any other character. As always with Flaubert, he combines individual features of different origin to form a new creation.

4 *Audran*: several members of the Audran family were engravers of note in the 17th and 18th centuries.

5 *thirty sous*: 1 franc 50, less than what she was to be paid per week by Madame Aubain.

6 *a substitute*: conscription was introduced in 1798, and all able-bodied men from 20 to 25 were liable, but a quota was fixed for each department and names were drawn by lot. Anyone who could afford it was allowed to pay a substitute to do his service, but his name could still come up again in subsequent years. Exemption was granted for several categories, including that of married men, and in fact rather less than half the men in each class were ever called up. As this incident is located in about 1809–10, at the height of the Napoleonic campaigns, Théodore's reluctance to serve, though not heroic, is at least understandable.

7 *Paul and Virginie*: Bernardin de Saint-Pierre's very successful novel of that name (1787) had made the two names a familiar brother-and-sister couple.
   boston: a fashionable card game for four players, something

like whist, reputedly invented during the siege of Boston in 1775.

11 *the Écores*: with the development of Trouville as a seaside resort this obstacle was removed.

12 *Mère David*: the name of a real person. *Mère* and *Père* are familiar, but not disrespectful, prefixes in French, and to avoid confusion with religious titles I have left them in the original.

godefiches: Flaubert uses this apparently rare dialect word without explanation. It seems to be an Anglicism, 'god-fish', referring to the scallop shells worn by pilgrims to Compostella and Mont-Saint-Michel.

15 *altar of repose*: the feast of Corpus Christi (*Fête-Dieu* in French) was instituted in the Middle Ages on the second Thursday after Pentecost, and the solemnity was celebrated in parishes on the Sunday following, as described at the end of the tale. Like the altar prepared on Maundy Thursday, on which this feast was modelled, it entailed careful decoration, but when it was celebrated by the whole population, temporary altars ('stations') were set up at various points from which Benediction of the Sacrament was given before the procession returned to church. The popular and spectacular nature of this summer festival was no doubt more striking to most people than its complex theological significance.

16 *those*: Flaubert underlined the word in the original.

18 *four leagues*: 16 kms.

19 *convent parlour*: in the original sense of the place in which outsiders could talk to the religious (or, as here, their pupils).

the Islands: the West Indies.

20 *an oval patch*: the map of Cuba.

26 *blessed bread*: a regular feature of Eastern liturgies, this survives in the West mostly in France. Originally a distribution of specially blessed bread to non-communicants, it is now offered to all at the end of the Eucharist as a sign of

fellowship, and is quite distinct from the consecrated bread. It was the custom for parishioners to provide this offering in turn.

the July Revolution: the ultra-royalist Comte d'Artois, brother of Louis XVI and Louis XVIII, came to the throne in 1824 as Charles X and was deposed after a brief revolution in July 1830, to be succeeded by his more liberal cousin, Louis-Philippe, Duc d'Orléans (deposed in his turn in 1848).

27 *the Poles*: a nationalist insurrection against Russian rule in Poland was finally crushed after some months in September 1831, and led to considerable emigration, particularly to France.

1793: at the height of the Revolutionary Terror (some forty years earlier!).

28 *Jacquot*: or *jaco*; from the 18th century, the popular name for the grey African (talking) parrot, later applied, like 'Poll', 'Polly' in English, as a generic name to all parrots.

30 *sacristy*: i.e. instead of in the confessional box in church.

31 *parsley*: a species of poisonous hemlock, resembling parsley closely enough to be confused with it, is in fact, called *faux-persil* (false parsley) in French.

32 *Saint-Gatien*: the scene in 1844 of Flaubert's first attack of pseudo-epilepsy while driving with his brother.

33 *the boat*: the packet-boat for Le Havre.

34 *the Comte d'Artois*: Charles X before he came to the throne in 1824 (see above); after his deposition his successor's portrait no doubt replaced his.

Children of Mary: a pious sodality for girls much younger than Félicité is at this point.

35 *Registration Office*: in French, *Enregistrement*, the administrative department dealing with the official registration of a wide range of deeds, wills, transfers, mortgages, and other documents attracting duty. There is no single British equivalent.

Dozulé: about 24 kms west of Pont-l'Évêque. Bourais's first mysterious absence had been noted much earlier, in about 1828.

39   *postillions*: often armed to protect the stage-coach from robbers. Military honours were often accorded to the Corpus Christi procession with the Sacrament, well within living memory.

SAINT JULIAN

42   *Amalekite*: the Amalekites were destroyed by Saul (1 Sam. 15), the Garamantes of the Fezzan are referred to by Virgil; like his mediaeval models, Flaubert is not concerned with consistency of time or place.

hennin: the steeple hat, sometimes with double points, and floating wings or panels, worn by fashionable ladies in the 15th century; it is crucially relevant to the final episode of this first section.

44   *Arabic . . . numbers*: as distinct from the cumbersome but universally used Roman system.

45   *pilgrim shells*: the scallop shells, *coquilles Saint-Jacques* named after Saint James of Compostella; see note to p. 12 above.

the Angelus service: strictly speaking, this brief devotion, consisting of repetition of the angelic salutation *Ave Maria*, followed by a prayer, is not a service at all, but during the Middle Ages the practice grew up of ringing a bell corresponding to the triple rhythm of the devotion after the evening office, then before the morning one and, rather later, at noon. As the famous picture by Millet shows, the bell served above all as a signal to those in the fields or distant from church. For some reason Flaubert both here and in *A Simple Heart* (p. 27) refers to the Angelus as a service (morning or evening) which people attend in church. Here it must mean the conclusion of the evening office.

46   *guide to the chase*: there were numerous such guides in the Middle Ages, of which *Le Livre du Roy Modus* is a particularly good example of question and answer method,

but Flaubert consulted a wide range, and a work by Gaston Phébus furnished much detail on hounds and hawks. The information is merely quoted, and not meant to be taken seriously. The exoticism of birds and beasts from Tartary and Central Asia (Alani), from the Caucasus and Babylon is in the original mediaeval source.

54 *Surena*: a title, meaning Grand Vizier, and not a proper name, despite Corneille's eponymous tragic hero in his last play. As before, it is pointless to seek historical or geographical significance in this catalogue of friends and foes.

the wyvern of Milan: the wyvern, or serpent, figures in the armorial bearings of the Sforza family (and the Visconti).

the dragon of Oberbirbach: this beast also seems to originate in armorial bearings, of a Count Frankestein, chosen for its Teutonic resonance by Flaubert in a compendious list of legends by A. Maury (1843, with later additions).

Occitania: though never a kingdom, the region where the 'langue d'oc' was spoken (and is being vigorously revived) is real enough, and centred on Toulouse.

61 *stinking beasts*: include badgers, polecats, martens.

70 *stained-glass window*: as mentioned in the Introduction, the window in Rouen Cathedral does indeed depict a number of episodes in the legend, but with numerous differences from the version composed by Flaubert.

HERODIAS

THE family relationships of the Herods are exceptionally complex, but essential to an understanding of the historical events underlying this story, and also the direct cause of John's clash with Antipas (and eventual death). The recurrence of the same names, and the flexible, to say the least, attitude towards tables of kindred and affinity within the family require explanation. The names of persons mentioned by Flaubert are italicized in the following note.

After some jockeying for position, *Herod the Great* was established King of Judaea with Roman backing in 37 BC and ruled until his death in 4 BC. He was an Edomite (Idumean, or Arab) by birth, but for political reasons found it convenient to support the Jewish religion, and built the last of the Temples in Jerusalem. He married Mariamne, grand-daughter of Hyrcan II, last of the Hasmonean (Maccabee) kings, and thus of impeccable Jewish stock, in 37 BC, but had her put to death in 29 BC through an obsessive jealousy which has inspired more than one drama. He had two sons by her, Alexander and Aristobulus, both killed on his orders in 7 BC. *Aristobulus* married Berenice, daughter of Herod's sister Salome, and had a daughter, *Herodias*, and a son, Herod *Agrippa*. The latter, who lived in Rome, fell out with the Emperor *Tiberius*, who imprisoned him for some six months in AD 37, but when Caligula (*Caius*) succeeded *Tiberius* late in that year, *Agrippa* was released, and assumed control of the Judaean territories as they fell vacant, with the title of King of Judaea, until his death in AD 44. His son, Agrippa II, did not take the title of king until AD 50, and then over the northern part of the territory only (Saint Paul's ruler in Acts 25).

In 23 BC *Herod the Great* married a second Mariamne, daughter of Simon of Alexandria, subsequently High Priest, and by her had a son, Herod *Philip*, whom he disowned, and who lived peaceably in Rome with no land to his name, and apparently no ambition. He married *Herodias* and their daughter was *Salome*.

After the death of the second Mariamne, *Herod* took seven more wives at different times. By Malthake, a Samaritan, he had two sons, *Archelaus* and *Antipas*, and by Cleopatra a son, confusingly called *Philip*. On *Herod*'s death the kingdom was divided between these three sons; *Archelaus* became Ethnarch of Judaea, Samaria and Idumaea, until deposed in AD 6 by the Romans, whereafter these territories were ruled by Roman procurators, of whom the best known was *Pontius Pilate*; *Antipas* became Tetrarch (originally ruler of the fourth part of a province, a subordinate title to king) of Galilee, until disgraced and banished, largely through the intrigues of *Agrippa*, in AD 39; *Philip* became Tetrarch of Batanaea (Basan) in the north-east, and ruled, apparently well, until his death in AD 34. Not long after John's execution, *c.* AD 30, this *Philip* married the *Salome* of our story. In spite of Flaubert's representation of their relationship, *Herodias* accompanied *Antipas* into exile (in the Pyrenees) and seems to have been loyal to him. They had been married in AD 27, after a double divorce, *Herodias* from Herod *Philip*, *Antipas* from the daughter of Aretas (Harith IV), King of the *Arabs*, or Nabateans, with his capital at Petra.

Finally it should be said that the political framework of the story involves antipathy between *Antipas* and the Roman Governor of Syria, *Vitellius*. The latter did not take up office until AD 35, and while all the incidents related (war with the Arabs, with the Parthians, disgrace of *Pilate* and much else) did actually happen, they all belong to the period after AD 35 and mostly to AD 37, shortly before *Antipas'* disgrace and exile. *Vitellius* had nothing to do with the death of John, or with that of Jesus.

It will be seen that Flaubert has used persons and events to construct from real facts a fictional variation on a historical theme. It would be tedious and wasteful of space to correct the details as they come up, and it is hoped that the foregoing may help to clarify issues which Flaubert's elliptic style tends to obscure.

71 *Machaerus*: the description of the fortress and the area to be seen from it is based on extensive reading, but as usual Flaubert improved on his sources (the walls, for example, are made much higher). French conventions for the transcription of Hebrew, Latin, and other languages are very different from those familiar to English readers, and where possible the form used in the Authorized Version of the Bible has been followed in this translation.

velarium: the awning for the roof terrace.

Carmel: not the famous Mount Carmel near Haifa.

Jericho: a long way south of Antipas' Galilee, but in the same direction looking out from Machaerus.

72 *Yemen*: general term for the whole Arabian peninsula; the former father-in-law did not in fact attack until AD 37.

73 *Samaritans*: Samaria had been the capital of the northern kingdom, Israel, but after the Assyrians had settled the area with pagans, the notably different religion practised at Gerizim became anathema to pious Jews, and Hyrcan I destroyed the temple there in 120 BC. Josephus is the source for the ritual defilement of the one in Jerusalem.

74   *For him to increase*: the quotation from John 3:30 is ironic
     in the story, but like the explanation of Iaokanann's name
     forcefully reminds the reader of the Gospels.

     cursed cities: Sodom and Gomorrah.

     cymar: a chimer, or loose gown.

75   *Caius*: Caligula.

     my daughter: more irony: the girl is only a few yards away,
     awaiting her instructions. Similarly the nostalgia for happier
     days long ago ignores the fact that they were married barely
     three years before Iaokanann's death.

76   *an Essene*: an ascetic Jewish secret society, associated with the
     Dead Sea scrolls. It used to be thought that John the Baptist
     (and even Jesus) was connected with them, as Phanuel clearly
     suggests, but modern scholarship rejects this theory.

     Nehemiah: the tradition that Elijah (Elias) would return,
     heralding the Messiah, goes back to about the 5th century
     BC.

78   *ancestral blood*: Herodias could indeed claim through her
     grandmother Mariamne descent from royal and priestly
     ancestors who had defeated and forcibly converted those
     of her husband; see introductory note.

81   *laticlave*: the name for the stripe in question, a badge of rank,
     like the escort of lictors.

     Clites: of Cilicia in Asia Minor.

     Aulus: this unprepossessing youth went on to occupy high
     office, and ruled for some months in AD 69 as Emperor
     (Vitellius), before being deposed and murdered by the mob.

     Herod the Great: the Athenians awarded him this honour
     after he had made a handsome donation to the games; the very
     pointed praise of Herod is Vitellius' oblique way of showing
     contempt for the son.

82   *Capri*: Tiberius' orgies at Capri and Aulus' status as one of the
     imperial playmates are well attested by Roman historians.

     High Priest: for some thirty years the politically and

religiously decisive office of High Priest was held by Sadducees, first Annas, deposed by the Romans, then his son-in-law Caiaphas (both familiar from the Passion story), deposed in his turn (by Vitellius) in AD 37 and succeeded by his son Jonathan. They differed from the Pharisees in accepting only the written Law, not oral tradition, and in their political and social orientation.

tiaras . . . strips of parchment: conical hats, as worn by early Popes, quite different from the modern beehive shape; the strips are the phylacteries, worn by pious Jews on forehead and arm (*Tephillin*).

83 *Pontius Pilate*: the incident occurred in Samaria in AD 36, and Pilate was then disgraced and exiled.

87 *Herod's treasure*: that of Herod the Great, as much of an obsession for the Romans as that of David for the Jews.

88 *Woe unto you . . .*: Iaokanann's words consist of a string of quotations, or paraphrases, from Scripture (including the New Testament), for which, it seems, Flaubert went to a French translation rather than the Vulgate or a translation thereof. The AV is different from both, and what follows is a translation of what Flaubert wrote, using the words of the AV wherever possible.

hyrax: the zoological name for the animal called 'cony' in the AV version of Psalm 104:18, *gerboise*, that is jerboa, by Flaubert, and 'rock-badger' in the NEB.

89 *kiccars*: the Hebrew equivalent of the more familiar 'talent', a unit of account and weight measure, worth 6,000 drachmas, while an obole was one sixth of a drachma; Flaubert plays deliberately on the linguistic babel of Palestine at the time by using a Hebrew and a Greek word in the same phrase.

a Son of David: the promised Messiah was to be of David's line which, of course, Antipas was not.

Ahab: husband of Jezebel, a byword for idolatrous and luxury-loving bad rulers, destroyed by Elijah; see 1 Kgs. 21–2.

incest: the Law regarded it as an act of charity to marry a deceased brother's wife, but Antipas had married by divorce the wife of a living half-brother who, moreover, had a child.

90   *chopines*: sandals with built-up soles.

91   *Absalom... Lot*: Antipas' knowledge of Scripture is as unimpressive as his sexual morality; all these examples come from Scripture, but are irrelevant, either because the deed was done unwittingly (Lot) or was harshly punished. Flaubert wrote Ammon for Amnon.

92   *Agalah ...*: Flaubert went to great length to check the position of the stars at the relevant time, and uses a mixture of Arabic, Hebrew, and Latin to identify them, stressing again the polyglot nature of the cultures present in Palestine.

93   *Polycleitus*: celebrated Greek sculptor of the 5th century BC; numerous copies of his work exist, e.g. in London and the Louvre.

94   *triclinium*: the couch extending round three sides of the dining table on which Romans reclined to eat.

95   *Simon of Gitta*: often identified with the Simon Magus of Acts 8, though not with certainty.

     chlamys: a kind of military cloak.

96   *ravens ... Zarephaph*: some of the more striking episodes in the life of Elias as reported in 1 Kgs. 17–19.

97   *nec crescit ...*: 'after death it [the body] does not grow, nor, as it seems, does it endure', according to Lucretius (died 55 BC).

     marble, schist ...: to calm his stomach and induce vomiting.

98   *Mithraic baptism*: the oriental cult of Mithras, which included a purification rite akin to baptism, was very popular at this time in the whole Roman world, especially among soldiers.

     Scandinavian headland: Asgard, abode of the gods, in Nordic mythology.

99   *Matathias*: leader of the Pharisees, executed by Herod the Great for opposing Roman rule.

100 *Moloch*: a vivid account of child sacrifice is to be found in

Salammbo, ch. 13. It obviously fascinated Flaubert.

Antigonus . . . Varus: they all came to a bad end, but not at the hands of the Jews.

mitre: a head-dress of stiff linen, probably quite different from modern episcopal headgear but, like *tiara*, put in to invite confusion.

101   *gingras*: a kind of flute.

103   *Aristobulus . . .*: this list of victims includes three of Herod's sons, and others closely connected with Mariamne and her supposed infidelity; in other words, people of some consequence, compared to this uncouth prophet.

The
Oxford
World's
Classics
Website

www.worldsclassics.co.uk

- Browse the full range of Oxford World's Classics online

- Sign up for our monthly e-alert to receive information on new titles

- Read extracts from the Introductions

- Listen to our editors and translators talk about the world's greatest literature with our Oxford World's Classics audio guides

- Join the conversation, follow us on Twitter at OWC_Oxford

- Teachers and lecturers can order inspection copies quickly and simply via our website

www.worldsclassics.co.uk

American Literature

British and Irish Literature

Children's Literature

Classics and Ancient Literature

Colonial Literature

Eastern Literature

European Literature

Gothic Literature

History

Medieval Literature

Oxford English Drama

Poetry

Philosophy

Politics

Religion

The Oxford Shakespeare

A complete list of Oxford World's Classics, including Authors in Context, Oxford English Drama, and the Oxford Shakespeare, is available in the UK from the Marketing Services Department, Oxford University Press, Great Clarendon Street, Oxford OX2 6DP, or visit the website at www.oup.com/uk/worldsclassics.

In the USA, visit www.oup.com/us/owc for a complete title list.

Oxford World's Classics are available from all good bookshops. In case of difficulty, customers in the UK should contact Oxford University Press Bookshop, 116 High Street, Oxford OX1 4BR.